Jean Rhys was born in Dominica in 1890, the daughter of a Welsh doctor and a white Creole mother. When she was sixteen she came to England, where, after her father died, she drifted into a series of demimonde jobs – chorus girl, mannequin, artist's model.

She began to write when the first of her three marriages broke up. She was in her thirties by then and living in Paris, where she was encouraged by Ford Madox Ford (who also discovered D. H. Lawrence). Ford wrote an enthusiastic introduction to her first book in 1927, a collection of stories called *The Left Bank*. This was followed by *Quartet* (originally *Postures*, 1928), *After Leaving Mr Mackenzie* (1930), *Voyage in the Dark* (1934) and *Good Morning, Midnight* (1939). None was particularly successful, no doubt because all were decades ahead of their time in theme and tone, dealing as they did with women as underdogs, exploited for, and exploiting, their sexuality. With the outbreak of war and subsequent failure of *Good Morning, Midnight*, the books went out of print, and Jean Rhys dropped completely out of sight. It was generally thought that she was dead. Nearly twenty years later she was rediscovered, largely due to the enthusiasm of the writer Francis Wyndham. She was living reclusively in Cornwall, and during those years had accumulated the stories collected in *Tigers are Better-Looking*. In 1966 she made a sensational reappearance with *Wide Sargasso Sea*, which won the Royal Society of Literature Award and the W. H. Smith Award for that year. Her only comment on her sudden great success was 'It has come too late'. Her final collection of stories, *Sleep It Off Lady*, appeared in 1976 and *Smile Please*, her unfinished autobiography, was published posthumously in 1979. She was made a Fellow of the Royal Society of Literature in 1966 and a CBE in 1978.

Jean Rhys, described by A. Alvarez as 'one of the finest British writers of this century', died in 1979.

Carole Angier is Jean Rhys's biographer. Her *Jean Rhys: Life and Work*, which appeared in 1990, was shortlisted for the Whitbread Biography Award and won the Writers' Guild Award for Non-Fiction. She is working on a biography of Primo Levi and is currently Royal Literary Fund Fellow at the

JEAN RHYS

Voyage in the Dark

With an Introduction by Carole Angier

PENGUIN BOOKS

PENGUIN BOOKS

Published by the Penguin Group
Penguin Books Ltd, 80 Strand, London WC2R 0RL, England
Penguin Putnam Inc., 375 Hudson Street, New York, New York 10014, USA
Penguin Books Australia Ltd, 250 Camberwell Road, Camberwell, Victoria 3124, Australia
Penguin Books Canada Ltd, 10 Alcorn Avenue, Toronto, Ontario, Canada M4V 3B2
Penguin Books India (P) Ltd, 11 Community Centre, Panchsheel Park, New Delhi – 110 017, India
Penguin Books (NZ) Ltd, Cnr Rosedale and Airborne Roads, Albany, Auckland, New Zealand
Penguin Books (South Africa) (Pty) Ltd, 24 Sturdee Avenue, Rosebank 2196, South Africa

Penguin Books Ltd, Registered Offices: 80 Strand, London WC2R 0RL, England

www.penguin.com

First published by Constable 1934
This edition published by André Deutsch 1967
Published in Penguin Books 1969
Reprinted with an Introduction in Penguin Classics 2000
10

Set in Baskerville Linotype
Printed in England by Clays Ltd, St Ives plc

ISBN-13: 978–0–141–18395–4

Introduction

When Jean Rhys wrote *Voyage in the Dark* in the early 1930s[1] she was in her early forties. She had returned to England from France, which she had sworn never to do. She made a second unhappy marriage; her daughter chose to live with her father, not with her; she fell into a deep pit of misery, and was drinking heavily. And yet this, her third novel, would be her youngest, warmest and most daring of all. That is the mystery of Jean Rhys.

I was so struck by her mystery that I became her biographer. That did not solve the mystery, of course, but confirmed it. It convinced me that, as well as universal works of art, Jean Rhys's novels were a quest for the truth about her own painful life. Behind each of them lies the question she gives to Antoinette in the last one, *Wide Sargasso Sea*: 'Why do such terrible things happen?' And with each her answer became more honest and less self-justifying. Jean Rhys's work, in other words, seemed to me not just a great artistic progress but a great moral one: a growing up she never managed in life.

In her two earlier novels she had set out two different answers to her question. The first, *Quartet*, was the story of an unhappy love affair, like *Voyage in the Dark* (and like *Voyage in the Dark*, based on one that had happened to her). For a first novel it is astoundingly good – as an artist Jean was born fully formed, like Pallas Athene from the forehead of Zeus. But it is flawed by her demon of self-pity. The heroine, Marya, sometimes seems to us selfish and cruel, but she never does to the novel. All the 'terrible things' that happen in *Quartet* are the man's fault, or the world's, never her own. Marya is Jean's first attempt at the heroine as innocent victim, and she fails.

Only two years later came *After Leaving Mr Mackenzie*, and Jean's second answer. Julia is no longer young and innocent; she is ageing, alcoholic and full of rage. She is Jean's first attempt at harsh honesty about her heroine; and her 'fifty-fifty lover', Mr Horsfield, Jean's first attempt at seeing a man's vulnerability, a man's point of view.

In the novel after *Voyage in the Dark*, Jean pursued her second answer: Sasha of *Good Morning, Midnight* plots a cruel revenge against men, and herself destroys her last chance of love. Finally, in *Wide Sargasso Sea*, the first answer returns – or rather, Jean finds an extraordinary resolution of the two. Antoinette is the maddest, most vengeful heroine of all: because, of course, she will become Bertha Rochester, the purple-faced destroyer of *Jane Eyre*. But in *Wide Sargasso Sea* itself she is an innocent victim, seen from inside: a child and little more than a child, broken by the hatreds in her own society, and by the encounter with a colder, harder one.

Anna of *Voyage in the Dark* belongs to this answer. She is young and innocent, abused and abandoned by a man – but a weak and vulnerable man like Julia's Mr Horsfield, not a monster of cruelty like Marya's Heidler. Anna is more than halfway to Antoinette, almost a rehearsal for Antoinette: a heroine we meet as a child in the West Indies; and if she never grows up, at least we know why. Until the great resolution of *Wide Sargasso Sea*, Anna was Jean Rhys's most successful innocent heroine, and she remained the most innocent of all. For that reason (I suspect) *Voyage in the Dark* was Jean's own favourite among her novels.[2]

After *Mackenzie*, Jean wrote to Francis Wyndham, her friend and future literary executor, 'the West Indies started knocking at my heart'.[3] That was the new element that would transform our understanding of the heroine: her West Indian childhood. Jean's first title for *Voyage in the Dark* reflected the importance of this new, or old, world in Anna's story: *Two Tunes*, two musics which neither she nor Anna could ever fit together.

By the end of 1931 she was 'very down', and put the novel aside. Finally she picked it up again some time in 1933, and finished it on 'two bottles of wine per day'.[4] Cape, who had published *Mackenzie*, turned it down. At last Michael Sadleir of Constable took it; but there was one last battle. He wanted to cut most of the final Part, Anna's stream-of-consciousness memories as her mind clouds; and – worst of all – he wanted Jean to change the ending. She was furious and frantic, but she did it. And Sadleir was right. Until Part IV she'd kept her (self-)pity for Anna under iron control, but in the end she'd let go: for in the original version, *Anna dies*. That made *Voyage in the Dark* a more clichéd and sentimental story. With Sadleir's change, the last trace of special pleading, of emotional blackmail of the reader, was removed; leaving a pure and perfect Jean Rhys novel.

Anna is halfway to Antoinette not only in her successful innocence, but in her whole strange, new, subversive point of view. This is the heart of Jean Rhys's daring, which is perhaps even greater in this novel than in *Wide Sargasso Sea*.

Antoinette's world is one of colour and sound, of light and dark, and of passionate, personal feeling – love, hate, happiness, fear. Rochester's – and Walter Jeffries' – England is its opposite: a grey world of conformity, of words and rules, of money, 'morality' and 'law'. 'Slavery was not a matter of liking or disliking,' Rochester says. 'It was a question of justice.' But to Antoinette 'words are no use', and all that matters is feeling. If there is liking, even slavery is just a word; if there is disliking, justice is less than a word, it is 'a damn cold lie'.[5]

That is already Anna's world, and Anna's feeling. Words and rules are meaningless to her. Morality is an advertisement on the back of a newspaper: 'What is Purity? For Thirty-five years the Answer has been Bourne's Cocoa.' All that matters is that when Walter kisses her, she is utterly happy. 'I am bad,' she thinks, 'not good any more, bad. That has no meaning, absolutely none. Just words.' Yet like Antoinette, on a deep, wordless level she knows what is waiting for her: '*But something about the darkness of the streets has a meaning.*'[6]

Now, the way that Jean tells Anna's story is the perfect expression of this wordless point of view. In *Quartet* she had tried (a little) to generalize from Marya's case, to seem to write for all underdogs, with their 'drably terrible [lives]'.[7] Not any more. She cut every 'objective' description, every logical connection, every general idea. We are wholly inside Anna: inside her feelings, her sensations, her memories; inside the vivid and sinister images that fill her mind. Even – especially – for her own acts there are no connections, and no explanations. As Uncle Bo says, 'She sent us a post-card from Blackpool or some such town and all she said on it was, "This is a very windy place," which doesn't tell us much about how she is getting on.'[8] When Walter drops her she disappears without leaving an address, though she hasn't a penny; she goes to Ethel, whom she fears and loathes, without telling herself, or us, why. It is like Antoinette's dream: '*This must happen.*'[9] And underneath it is like Julia's rage, and Sasha's revenge: desperate, self-punishing pride. 'You must have known that Walter would look after you,' Vincent says. 'So much every Saturday,' Anna replies bitterly. 'Receipt form enclosed.'[10]

Jean Rhys was a writer who distrusted words. She used the fewest and shortest ones she could, as though she were trying not to use words at all: *Voyage in the Dark*, she said, was written 'almost entirely in words of one syllable. Like a kitten mewing'.[11] She put her meaning in what she does not

viii

say (she does not say 'bitterly', for example, in the exchange above), and in what her characters do not say ('Are you sure these are all the letters?' Vincent asks, removing all traces of Walter's affair. 'I've told you so,' Anna replies. 'Well, there you are, I'm trusting you,' he says. 'Yes,' Anna says, 'I see that.'[12]) She put her meaning behind the words, like the menace all the heroines feel 'under the more or less pleasant surface of things.'[13] And since it lurks hidden and wordless for us, as it does for them, we feel it in the same hidden and wordless way.

We read *Voyage in the Dark* like this because we must, because that is how it is written. But Jean also tells us that that is how we should read it: or rather, she hints that that is how we should read it, through images of meaning. The first comes right at the start, in the first thing we see Anna do: she is reading a book 'about a tart',[14] as Maudie says – which is, in cold external words, what we are doing too. And this is what Anna says about her reading:

The print was very small, and the endless procession of words gave me a curious feeling – sad, excited and frightened. It wasn't what I was reading, it was the look of the dark, blurred words going on endlessly that gave me that feeling.[15]

That is how we must read *Voyage in the Dark*: attending to 'looks' and 'feelings', not to the words, which belong to the powerful, like the laws (and that, of course, is why Jean Rhys distrusts them).

The second image of meaning comes in one of Anna's memories of the West Indies: which is precisely right, because the difference in Anna's way of meaning (and Antoinette's, and Jean Rhys's) is the difference between childhood and adulthood, between feeling and reasoning, between the West Indies and England. Anna's stepmother Hester is the arch-Englishwoman, cold, snobbish and disapproving. Francine was the black servant girl of Anna's childhood, who made her feel safe and happy, who made her want to be black. And this is Anna's memory:

> [Hester] always hated Francine.
> 'What do you talk about?' she used to say.
> 'We don't talk about anything,' I'd say. 'We just talk.'
> But she didn't believe me.[16]

White people think that words mean what they say – what the words say. Jean Rhys knows they mean what they, the white people, say. Black people talk as they sing and laugh, to share their feelings; and they know that people, not words, mean things. That is the radical idea of meaning that informs *Voyage in the Dark*.

With all rational explanation cut, with the past as real as the present, *Voyage in the Dark* is close to poetry. And the main bearer of its meaning is a poetic one: imagery.

At each stage of Anna's affair the truth about it appears in an image. When it begins she sees a couple kissing: and rather than beautiful and happy they are sad and sinister, 'like beetles clinging to the railings.'[17] When she sees the letter that will end it on her table, she remembers something that happened years ago: coming upon her favourite uncle asleep on the verandah, his mouth open.

> . . . Uncle Bo moved and sighed and long yellow tusks like fangs came out of his mouth and protruded down to his chin – you don't scream when you are frightened because you can't and you don't move either because you can't . . .[18]

'What the hell's the matter with me?' she thinks. 'This letter has nothing to do with false teeth.'[19] But it has everything to do with a beloved face suddenly sprouting cruel fangs against you. This is what Anna has feared from the start, what she has always known would happen: 'I'd been afraid for a long time, I'd been afraid for a long time . . .'.[20]

The beetle-lovers and snake-uncle are part of a whole system of animal imagery in the novel. Ethel, the nastiest person of all, is an ant, ready to transform into a still more sinister and efficient insect: 'Feelers grow when feelers are needed and claws when claws are needed and cunning when cunning is needed . . .'[21] Crabs lurked in the bathing pool of Anna's childhood, like the monster crab in *Wide Sargasso Sea*;[22] barracuda lurked in the sea, 'flat-headed, sharp-toothed', 'swimming by the side of the boat, waiting to snap.'[23] Plants and trees, too, bulge with meaning. The shiny spiky red rubber plant expresses the smug hostility of Anna's boarding house;[24] trees throughout the story express her own state of mind – lopped, 'like a man with stumps instead of arms and legs', before she meets Walter; 'perfectly still, as if it were dead',[25] when their affair is over. ('Why did you make me want to live?' Antoinette asks Rochester. 'Why did you do that to me?'[26])

England, the apotheosis of power and possession, both everything Anna longs for – protection, security – and everything she fears – rejection, exclusion – England is a high, dark wall. English voices are 'high, smooth, un-climbable walls',[27] the look in Vincent's eyes is like 'a high, smooth, unclimbable wall. No communication possible.'[28] All of this – the desired protection, the dreaded rejection – is summed up in another image, another memory: the picture on the English biscuit tin at home in the West Indies. A little boy, a little girl, a green tree, a blue sky; and behind the little girl a high, dark wall. 'And that used to be my idea of what England was like,' Anna says[29] – thinking, we guess, of the safety and solidity of that high wall. 'And it is like that, too,' she thinks: with her, we know, on the other side of the wall.

This flight from words to pictures is not just the perfect expression of Jean Rhys's distrust of language, which some-one else owns: *it works*. As long as she said things about society, about people, we could resist her, as we do in *Quartet*. But these fearful, enigmatic images slip under our conscious guard, and persuade us before we have noticed. Her genius was to cut everything she did less well, and use them.

Anna is Jean Rhys's most innocent heroine, but she is not as innocent as all that. She is extraordinarily passive, then suddenly, violently proud – turning on Laurie, jamming her cigarette on Walter's hand. She is only nineteen, but she is already starting to drink ('I should go slow on the gin,' Laurie says, 'You've been taking too much lately.'[30]) And something else is starting too. When a man speaks to her on the street, she wants to hit him, and nearly does. 'What happened to me then?' she thinks. 'Something happened to me then?'[31] What happened is that she has already moved from hurt child to vengeful woman; from herself to Julia, Sasha and Antoinette.

And if *Voyage in the Dark*'s heroine is not unbelievably good, its villains are not unbelievably bad. When they *are* bad, they are utterly believable: Hester, Ethel and Vincent are so well observed we cannot doubt for a moment their smug, self-protective cruelty; and Vincent's and Ethel's letters are masterpieces of (respectively) smiling and spitting betrayal. But the other villains of the piece are hardly villains at all: Carl and Joe, who meet Anna as a tart and treat her as one, but who are decent, ordinary men, with struggles of their own ('Nobody wins,' Carl says, 'Don't worry. Nobody wins'[32]); above all, Walter, whose abandonment of Anna 'smashes her up', as Marya was smashed up by Heidler, and Julia by Mr Mackenzie.[33] Walter is cautious, cowardly and weak, he lets Vincent do his dirty work, and worries more about his health than about Anna. But he is more than half on Anna's side; and like Rochester with Antoinette, briefly he forgets caution ('Shy Anna, I love you so much. Always, Walter.'[34]) Walter was based on the one man Jean truly loved; and that glimpse of the possibility of love – as much hers for another human being as his for her – produces her best balance. If you respond to her dark vision of haves and have-nots, of masters and slaves, you will want to read everything she wrote. But if you will only ever read one of her novels, I recommend this one.

NOTES

1. *After Leaving Mr Mackenzie* was published in February 1931. Jean was certainly working on *Voyage in the Dark* by June 1931: *vide* her letter to Evelyn Scott, 23 June 1931, in *Jean Rhys Letters, 1931–1966*, edited by Francis Wyndham and Diana Melly (André Deutsch, 1984), p. 21.

2. See her interviews with Nan Robertson ('Jean Rhys: the Voyage of a Writer', *New York Times*, 25 January 1978) and Elizabeth Vreeland ('Jean Rhys', *Paris Review*, Fall 1979); 'The Hole in the Curtain' ('Het Gaatje in het Gordijn') by Jan van Houts, *Zaandam*, October 1981, translated by John Rudge; draft for *Smile Please*, dated 14 March 1974, now in the Jean Rhys Collection, McFarlin Library, University of Tulsa.

3. Jean Rhys to Francis Wyndham, 14 September 1959, *Letters*, p. 171.

4. Jean Rhys to Evelyn Scott, 18 February 1934, *Letters*, p. 23.

5. *Wide Sargasso Sea*, Penguin, pp. 111 ('words are no use') and 121.

6. *Voyage in the Dark*, Penguin, pp. 49 and 50. Last emphasis mine.

7. *Quartet*, Penguin, p. 85. See also, for example, pp. 31, 44, 98.

8. *Voyage in the Dark*, p. 53.

9. *Wide Sargasso Sea*, p. 50. (My emphasis.)

10. *Voyage in the Dark*, p. 147.

11. Jean Rhys to Evelyn Scott, 18 February 1934, *Letters* p. 24.

12. *Voyage in the Dark*, p. 149.

13. *Quartet*, p. 28.

14. *Voyage in the Dark*, p. 9.

15. Ibid. p. 9.

16. Ibid. p. 58.

17. Ibid. p. 30.

18. Ibid. p. 79.

19. Ibid. p. 81.

20. Ibid. p. 82.

21. Ibid. pp. 91 (Ethel as an ant) and 92.

22. Ibid. p. 78 and *Wide Sargasso Sea*, pp. 73–4.

23. *Voyage in the Dark*, p. 46.

24. Ibid. p. 30.

25. Ibid. pp. 9 and 144.

26. *Wide Sargasso Sea*, p. 77.

27. *Voyage in the Dark*, p. 126.

28. Ibid. p. 147.

29. Ibid. p. 127 (also following quote).

30. Ibid. p. 152.

31. Ibid. p. 126.

32. Ibid. p. 132.

33. The phrase comes from *After Leaving Mr Mackenzie* (see Penguin, p. 37).

34. *Voyage in the Dark*, p. 148. For *Wide Sargasso Sea*, see p. 76.

Part One

I

It was as if a curtain had fallen, hiding everything I had ever known. It was almost like being born again. The colours were different, the smells different, the feeling things gave you right down inside yourself was different. Not just the difference between heat, cold; light, darkness; purple, grey. But a difference in the way I was frightened and the way I was happy. I didn't like England at first. I couldn't get used to the cold. Sometimes I would shut my eyes and pretend that the heat of the fire, or the bed-clothes drawn up round me, was sun-heat; or I would pretend I was standing outside the house at home, looking down Market Street to the Bay. When there was a breeze the sea was millions of spangles; and on still days it was purple as Tyre and Sidon. Market Street smelt of the wind, but the narrow street smelt of niggers and wood-smoke and salt fishcakes fried in lard. (When the black women sell fishcakes on the savannah they carry them in trays on their heads. They call out, 'Salt fishcakes, all sweet an charmin', all sweet an' charmin'.') It was funny, but that was what I thought about more than anything else – the smell of the streets and the smells of frangipanni and lime juice and cinnamon and cloves, and sweets made of ginger and syrup, and incense after funerals or Corpus Christi processions, and the patients standing outside the surgery next door, and the smell of the sea-breeze and the different smell of the land-breeze.

Sometimes it was is if I were back there and as if

England were a dream. At other times England was the real thing and out there was the dream, but I could never fit them together.

After a while I got used to England and I liked it all right; I got used to everything except the cold and that the towns we went to always looked so exactly alike. You were perpetually moving to another place which was perpetually the same. There was always a little grey street leading to the stage-door of the theatre and another little grey street where your lodgings were, and rows of little houses with chimneys like the funnels of dummy steamers and smoke the same colour as the sky; and a grey stone promenade running hard, naked and straight by the side of the grey-brown or grey-green sea; or a Corporation Street or High Street or Duke Street or Lord Street where you walked about and looked at the shops.

Southsea, this place was.

We had good rooms. The landlady had said, 'No, I don't let to professionals.' But she didn't bang the door in our faces, and after Maudie had talked for a while, making her voice sound as ladylike as possible, she had said, 'Well, I might make an exception for this time.' Then the second day we were there she made a row because we both got up late and Maudie came downstairs in her nightgown and a torn kimono.

'Showing yourself at my sitting-room-window 'alf naked like that,' the landlady said. 'And at three o'clock in the afternoon too. Getting my house a bad name.'

'It's all right, ma,' Maudie said. 'I'm going up to get dressed in a minute. I had a shocking headache this morning.'

'Well, I won't 'ave it,' the landlady said. 'When you come downstairs for your dinner you've got to be decent. Not in your nightclothes.'

She slammed the door.

'I ask you,' Maudie said, 'I ask you. That old goat's

starting to get on my nerves. I'll tell her off if she says another word to me.'

'Don't take any notice of her,' I said.

I was lying on the sofa, reading *Nana*. It was a paper-covered book with a coloured picture of a stout, dark woman brandishing a wine-glass. She was sitting on the knee of a bald-headed man in evening dress. The print was very small, and the endless procession of words gave me a curious feeling – sad, excited and frightened. It wasn't what I was reading, it was the look of the dark, blurred words going on endlessly that gave me that feeling.

There was a glass door behind the sofa. You could see into a small, unfurnished room, and then another glass door led into the walled-in garden. The tree by the back wall was lopped so that it looked like a man with stumps instead of arms and legs. The washing hung limp, without moving, in the grey-yellow light.

'I'll get dressed,' Maudie said, 'and then we'd better go out and get some air. We'll go to the theatre and see if there are any letters. That's a dirty book, isn't it?'

'Bits of it are all right,' I said.

Maudie said, 'I know; it's about a tart. I think it's disgusting. I bet you a man writing a book about a tart tells a lot of lies one way and another. Besides, all books are like that – just somebody stuffing you up.'

Maudie was tall and thin, and her nose made a straight line with her forehead. She had pale yellow hair and a very white, smooth skin. When she smiled a tooth was missing on one side. She was twenty-eight years old and all sorts of things had happened to her. She used to tell me about them when we came back from the theatre at night. 'You've only got to learn how to swank a bit, then you're all right,' she would say. Lying in bed with her, her hair in two long yellow plaits on either side of her long white face.

'Swank's the word,' she would say.

9

There were no letters for us at the theatre.

Maudie said she knew a shop where I could get a pair of stockings I wanted. 'That street just before you get on to the front,' she said.

Somebody was playing the piano in one of the houses we passed – a tinkling sound like water running. I began to walk very slowly because I wanted to listen. But it got farther and farther away and then I couldn't hear it any more. 'Gone for ever,' I thought. There was a tight feeling in my throat as if I wanted to cry.

'There's one thing about you,' Maudie said. 'You always look ladylike.'

'Oh God,' I said, 'who wants to look ladylike?'

We walked on.

'Don't look round,' Maudie said. 'Two men are following us. I think they're trying to get off with us.'

The two men went past and walked ahead very slowly. One of them had his hands in his pockets; I liked the way he walked. It was the other one, the taller one, who looked back and smiled.

Maudie giggled.

'Good afternoon,' he said. 'Are you going for a walk? Nice day, isn't it? Very warm for October.'

'Yes, we're taking the air,' Maudie said. 'Not all of it, of course.'

Everybody laughed. We paired off. Maudie went on ahead with the tall man. The other looked at me sideways once or twice – very quickly up and down, in that way they have – and then asked where we were going.

'I was going to this shop to buy a pair of stockings,' I said.

They all came into the shop with me. I said I wanted two pairs – lisle thread with clocks up the sides – and took a long time choosing them. The man I had been walking with offered to pay for them and I let him.

When we got outside Maudie said, 'Gone quite chilly,

hasn't it? Why don't you two come back to our rooms and have some tea? We live quite near by.'

The tall man seemed rather anxious to get away, but the other one said they would like to; and they bought two bottles of port and some cakes on the way back.

We had no latch-key. I thought the landlady would be sure to be rude when she let us in. However, when she opened the door she only glared, without speaking.

The fire was laid in the sitting-room. Maudie put a match to it and lit the gas. On the mantelpiece two bronze horses pawed the air with their front legs on either side of a big, dark clock. Blue plates hung round the walls at regular intervals.

'Make yourselves at home, you blokes,' Maudie said. 'And allow me to introduce Miss Anna Morgan and Miss Maudie Beardon, now appearing in *The Blue Waltz*. What about opening the port? I'll get you a corkscrew, Mr What's-your-name. What is your name, by the way?'

The tall man didn't answer. He stared over her shoulder, his eyes round and opaque. The other one coughed.

Maudie said in cockney, 'I was speaking to you, 'Orace. You 'eard. You ain't got clorf ears. I asked what your name was.'

'Jones,' the tall man said. 'Jones is my name.'

'Go on,' Maudie said.

He looked annoyed.

'That's rather funny,' the other one said, starting to laugh.

'What's funny?' I said.

'You see, Jones is his name.'

'Oh, is it?' I said.

He stopped laughing. 'And my name's Jeffries.'

'Is it really?' I said. 'Jeffries, is it?'

'Jones and Jeffries,' Maudie said. 'That's not hard to remember.'

I hated them both. You pick up people and then they are rude to you. This business of picking up people and then they always imagine they can be rude to you.

But when I had had a glass of port I began to laugh too and after that I couldn't stop. I watched myself in the glass over the mantelpiece, laughing.

'How old are you?' Mr Jeffries said.

'I'm eighteen. Did you think I was older?'

'No,' he said. 'On the contrary.'

Mr Jones said, 'He knew you'd be either eighteen or twenty-two. You girls only have two ages. You're eighteen and so of course your friend's twenty-two. Of course.'

'You're one of those clever people, aren't you?' Maudie said, sticking her chin out. She always did that when she was vexed. 'You know everything.'

'Well, I am eighteen,' I said. 'I can show you my birth certificate if you like.'

'No, my dear child, no. That would be excessive,' Mr Jones said.

He brought the bottle of port over and filled my glass again. When he touched my hand he pretended to shiver. He said, 'Oh God, cold as ice. Cold and rather clammy.'

'She's always cold,' Maudie said. 'She can't help it. She was born in a hot place. She was born in the West Indies or somewhere, weren't you, kid? The girls call her the Hottentot. Isn't it a shame?'

'Why the Hottentot?' Mr Jeffries said. 'I hope you call them something worse back.'

He spoke very quickly, but with each word separated from the other. He didn't look at my breasts or my legs, as they usually do. Not that I saw. He looked straight at me and listened to everything I said with a polite and attentive expression, and then he looked away and smiled as if he had sized me up.

He asked how long I had been in England, and I told him, 'Two years,' and then we talked about the tour. The company was going on to Brighton, then Eastbourne, and then we finished in London.

'London?' Mr Jones said, lifting his eyebrows.

'Well, Holloway. Holloway's London, isn't it?'

'Of course it is,' Mr Jeffries said.

'That's enough about the show,' Maudie said. She still looked vexed. 'Tell us about yourselves for a change. Tell us how old you are and what you do for a living. Just for a change.'

Mr Jeffries said. 'I work in the City. I work very hard.'

'You mean somebody else works hard for you,' Maudie said. 'And what does Daniel-in-the-lions'-den do? But it's no use asking him. He won't tell us. Cheer up, Daniel, d'you know the one about the snake-charmer?'

'No, I don't think I know that one,' Mr Jones said stiffly.

Maudie told the one about the snake-charmer. They didn't laugh much, and then Mr Jones coughed and said they had to go.

'I wish we could have seen your show tonight,' Mr Jeffries said, 'but I'm afraid it's not possible. We must meet again when you come up to London; yes, certainly we must meet again.'

'Perhaps you would dine with me one evening, Miss Morgan,' he said. 'Will you give me an address that'll find you, so that we can fix it up?'

I said, 'We'll be at Holloway in a fortnight, but this is my permanent address.' I wrote down:

> Miss Anna Morgan
> c/o Mrs Hester Morgan,
> 118, Fellside Road,
> Ilkley,
> Yorks.

'Is that your mother?'

'No, Hester's my stepmother.'

'We must fix it up,' he said. 'I shall look forward to it.'

We went out into the street to say good-bye to them. I was thinking it was funny I could giggle like that because in my heart I was always sad, with the same sort of hurt that the cold gave me in my chest.

We went back into the sitting-room. We heard the landlady coming along the passage outside.

'She's going to make another row,' Maudie said.

We listened. But she passed the door without coming in.

Maudie said, 'What I'd like to know is this: why they think they've got the right to insult you for nothing at all? That's what I'd like to know.'

I got very close to the fire. I was thinking, 'It's October. Winter's coming.'

'You got off with your bloke,' Maudie said. 'Mine was a bit of no good. Did you hear what he said about my being twenty-two and sort of sneering?'

'I didn't like either of them,' I said.

'You gave your address pretty quick, though,' Maudie said. 'And quite right too. You go out with him if he asks you. Those men have money; you can tell that in a minute, can't you? Anybody can. Men who have money and men who haven't are perfectly different.

'I've never seen anybody shiver like you do,' she said. 'It's awful. Do you do it on purpose or what? Get on the sofa and I'll put my big coat over you if you like.'

The coat had a warm animal smell and a cheap scent smell.

'Viv gave me that coat,' Maudie said. 'He's like that. He doesn't give much but what he gives is good stuff, not shoddy.'

'Like a Jew,' I said. 'Is he a Jew?'

'Of course he isn't. I told you.'

She went on talking about the man who gave her the

coat. His name was Vivian Roberts and she had been in love with him for a long time. She still saw him when she was up in London between tours, but only very occasionally. She said she was sure he was breaking it off, but doing it gradually because he was cautious and he did everything gradually.

She went on talking about him. I didn't listen.

Thinking how cold the street would be outside and the dressing-room cold too, and that my place was by the door in the draught. It always was. A damned shame. And about Laurie Gaynor, who was dressing next me that week. The virgin, she calls me, or sometimes the silly cow. ('Can't you manage to keep the door shut, Virgin, you silly cow?') But I like her better than any of the others. She's a fine girl. She's the only one I really like. And the cold nights; and the way my collar-bones stick out in my first-act dress. There's something you can buy that makes your neck fat. Venus Carnis. 'No fascination without curves. Ladies, realize your charms.' But it costs three guineas and where can I get three guineas? And the cold nights, the damned cold nights.

Lying between 15° 10′ and 15° 40′ N. and 61° 14′ and 61° 30′ W. A goodly island and something highland, but all overgrown with woods,' that book said. And all crumpled into hills and mountains as you would crumple a piece of paper in your hand – rounded green hills and sharply-cut mountains.

A curtain fell and then I was here.

... This is England Hester said and I watched it through the train-window divided into squares like pocket-hand-kerchiefs; a small tidy look it had everywhere fenced off from everywhere else – what are those things – those are haystacks – oh are those haystacks – I had read about England ever since I could read – smaller meaner every-thing is never mind – this is London – hundreds thou-sands of white people white people rushing along and the dark houses all alike frowning down one after the other all alike all stuck together – the streets like smooth shut-in ravines and the dark houses frowning down – oh I'm not going to like this place I'm not going to like this place I'm not going to like this place – you'll get used to it Hester kept saying I expect you feel like a fish out of water but you'll soon get used to it – now don't look like Dying Dick and Solemn Davy as your poor father used to say you'll get used to it ...

Maudie said, 'Let's finish the port.' She poured out two glasses and we drank slowly. She watched herself in the mirror.

'I'm getting lines under my eyes, aren't I?'

I said, 'I've got a cousin out home, quite a kid. And she's never seen snow and she's awfully curious about it. She keeps writing and asking me to tell her what it's like. I wanted to see snow, too. That was one of the things I was longing to see.'

'Well,' Maudie said, 'you've seen it now, haven't you? How much do you suppose our bill's going to be this week?'

'About fifteen bob, I suppose.'

We reckoned up.

I had saved six pounds and Hester had promised to send me five pounds for Christmas, or earlier if I wanted it. So I had decided to find a cheap room somewhere instead of going to the chorus-girls' hostel in Maple Street. A ghastly place, that was.

'Only three more weeks of this damned tour, T.G.,' Maudie said. 'It's no life, not in winter it isn't.'

When we were coming home from the theatre that night it began to rain and in Brighton it rained all the time. We got to Holloway and it was winter and the dark streets round the theatre made me think of murders.

I gave Maudie the letter to read and she said, 'I told

you so. I told you he had money. That's an awfully swanky club. The four swankiest clubs in London are ...'

All the girls started arguing about which was the swankiest club in London.

I wrote and said I couldn't dine with him on Monday, because I had a previous engagement. ('Always say you have a previous engagement.') But I said I could on Wednesday, the 17th of November, and I gave him the address of the room I had taken in Judd Street.

Laurie Gaynor said, 'Tell him to borrow the club tin-opener. Say "P.S. Don't forget the tin-opener".'

'Oh, leave her alone,' Maudie said.

'That's all right,' Laurie said. 'I'm not troubling her. I'm teaching her etiquette.'

'She knows I'm a good old cow,' Laurie said. 'A lot better than most of the other old cows. Aren't I, what's-your-name – Anna?'

2

I looked down at my hands and the nails shone as bright as brass. At least, the left hand did – the right wasn't so good.

'Do you always wear black?' he said. 'I remember you were wearing a black dress when I saw you before.'

'Wait a minute,' he said. 'Don't drink that.'

The waiter knocked a long, elaborate knock and came in to take away the soup.

'This wine is corked,' Mr Jeffries said.

'Corked, sir?' the waiter said in a soft, incredulous and horror-stricken voice. He had a hooked nose and a pale, flat face.

'Yes, corked. Smell that.'

The waiter sniffed. Then Mr Jeffries sniffed. Their

noses were exactly alike, their faces very solemn. The Brothers Slick and Slack, the Brothers Pushmeofftheearth. I thought, 'Now then, you mustn't laugh. He'll know you're laughing at him. You can't laugh.'

There was a red-shaded lamp on the table, and heavy pink silk curtains over the windows. There was a hard, straight-backed sofa, and two chairs with curved legs against the wall – all upholstered in red. The Hoffner Hotel and Restaurant, the place was called. The Hoffner Hotel and Restaurant, Hanover Square.

The waiter finished apologizing and went out. Then he came in again with the fish and another bottle of wine and filled up our glasses. I drank mine quickly because all day I had been feeling as if I had caught a cold. I had a pain in my throat.

'How's your friend – Maisie?'

'Maudie.'

'Yes, Maudie. How's Maudie?'

'Oh, she's all right,' I said. 'She's very well.'

'What's become of her? Is she still with you?'

'No,' I said. 'Between tours she stays with her mother in Kilburn.'

He said, 'She stays with her mother in Kilburn, does she?' and looked at me as if he were trying to size me up. 'What do you do between tours as a rule? Do you stay with the lady whose address you gave me?'

'My stepmother?' I said. 'Hester? No, I don't see much of her. She's not often in London.'

'Do you always stay at those rooms in Judd Street?'

'Room,' I said, 'room. There's only one. No. I've never been there before and I don't like it much. But it's better than the Cats' Home, anyway. That's where I was last summer – the chorus-girls' hostel in Maple Street. It got on my nerves because they make you come down to prayers every morning before breakfast.'

I drank some more wine and stared at the table-cloth,

seeing the matron praying with uplifted face and shut eyes. And her little, short nose and her long, moving lips. Just like a rabbit, she was, like a blind rabbit. There was something horrible about that sort of praying. I thought, 'I believe there's something horrible about any sort of praying.'

I saw her and I saw the shadows of the carnations that were on the table and we talked about touring and he asked me how much I was getting. I told him, 'Thirty-five bob a week, and of course extra for extra matinées.'

'Good God,' he said. 'You surely can't manage on that, can you?'

'I'm getting along all right,' I thought. But the waiter coming in and out, bringing us things to eat, bothered me.

We had another bottle of wine and I felt it warm and happy in my stomach. I heard my voice going on and on, answering his questions, and all the time I was talking he kept looking at me in a funny sort of way, as if he didn't believe what I was saying.

'So you don't see much of your stepmother? Doesn't she approve of your gadding about on tour? Does she think you've disgraced the family or something?'

I looked at him, and he was smiling as if he were laughing at me. I stopped talking. I thought, 'Oh God, he's the sneering sort. I wish I hadn't come.'

But when the waiter brought in coffee and liqueurs and shut the door as if he wasn't coming back and we went over to the fire, I felt all right again. I liked the room and the red carnations on the table and the way he talked and his clothes – especially his clothes. It was a pity about my clothes, but anyway they were black. 'She wore black. Men delighted in that sable colour, or lack of colour.' A man called 'Coronet' wrote that, or was it a man called 'A Peer'?

He said, 'You've got the loveliest teeth. You're sweet.

19

You looked awfully pathetic when you were choosing those horrible stockings so anxiously.' And then he started kissing me and all the time he was kissing me I was thinking about the man at that supper-party at the Greyhound, Croydon, when he told me, 'You don't know how to kiss. I'll show you how to kiss. This is what you do.'

I felt giddy. I twisted my head away and got up.

There was a door behind the sofa, but I hadn't noticed it before because a curtain hung over it. I turned the handle. 'Oh,' I said, 'it's a bedroom.' My voice went high.

'So it is,' he said. He laughed. I laughed too, because I felt that that was what I ought to do. *You can now and you can see what it's like, and why not?*

My arms hung straight down by my sides awkwardly. He kissed me again, and his mouth was hard, and I remembered him smelling the glass of wine and I couldn't think of anything but that, and I hated him.

'Look here, let me go,' I said. He said something I didn't hear. 'Do you think I was born yesterday, or what?' I said, talking very loud. I pushed him away as hard as I could. I could feel the sharp points of his collar against my hand. I kept saying, 'Damn you, let me go, damn you. Or I'll make a hell of a row.' But as soon as he let me go I stopped hating him.

'I'm very sorry,' he said. 'That was extremely stupid of me.' Looking at me with his eyes narrow and close together, as if he hated me, as if I wasn't there; and then he turned away and looked at himself in the glass.

There were the red carnations on the table and the fire leaping up. I thought, 'If it could go back and be just as it was before it happened and then happen differently.'

I took up my coat and hat and went into the bedroom. I pushed the door shut after me.

There was a fire but the room was cold. I walked up to

the looking-glass and put the lights on over it and stared at myself. It was as if I were looking at somebody else. I stared at myself for a long time, listening for the door to open. But I didn't hear a sound from the next room. There wasn't a sound from anywhere. When I listened I could only hear a noise like when you hold a shell up to your ear, like something rushing past you.

In this room too the lights were shaded in red; and it had a secret feeling – quiet, like a place where you crouch down when you are playing hide-and-seek.

I sat down on the bed and listened, then I lay down. The bed was soft; the pillow was as cold as ice. I felt as if I had gone out of myself, as if I were in a dream.

Soon he'll come in again and kiss me, but differently. He'll be different and so I'll be different. It'll be different. I thought, 'It'll be different, different. It must be different.'

I lay there for a long while, listening. The fire was like a painted fire; no warmth came from it. When I put my hand against my face it was very cold and my face was hot. I began to shiver. I got up and went back into the next room.

'Hullo,' he said, 'I thought you'd gone to sleep.'

He smiled at me, as cool as a cucumber. 'Cheer up,' he said. 'Don't look so sad. What's the matter? Have another kümmel.'

'No, thank you,' I said. 'I don't want anything.' My chest hurt.

We stood there looking at each other. He said, 'Come on, let's go, for God's sake,' and held my coat up for me. I got into it and put my hat on.

We went down the stairs.

I was thinking, 'The girls would shriek with laughter if I were to tell them this. Simply shriek.'

We went out into the street and walked to the corner and he stopped a taxi. 'Let's see – Judd Street, isn't it?'

I got into the taxi. He gave the driver some money.

'Well, good night.'

'Good night,' I said.

It was early when I got back, not twelve o'clock. I had a little room on the second floor. Ten-and-six a week I paid for it.

I undressed and got into bed, but I couldn't get warm. The room had a cold, close smell. It was like being in a small, dark box.

Somebody went past in the street, singing. Bawling:

> 'Bread, bread, bread,
>   Standard bread,
> A little bit er Standard bread,
>   Pom, pom,'

over and over again.

I thought, 'What a song! Mad as a hatter that song is. It's the tune that's so awful; it's like blows.' But the words went over and over again in my head and I began to breathe in time to them.

When I thought about my clothes I was too sad to cry.

About clothes, it's awful. Everything makes you want pretty clothes like hell. People laugh at girls who are badly dressed. Jaw, jaw, jaw. ... 'Beautifully dressed woman. ... As if it isn't enough that you want to be beautiful, that you want to have pretty clothes, that you want it like hell. As if that isn't enough. But no, it's jaw, jaw and sneer, sneer all the time. And the shop-windows sneering and smiling in your face. And then you look at the skirt of your costume, all crumpled at the back. And your hideous underclothes. You look at your hideous underclothes and you think, 'All right, I'll do anything for good clothes. Anything – anything for clothes.'

'But it isn't always going to be like this, is it?' I thought.

'It would be too awful if it were always going to be like this. It isn't possible. Something must happen to make it different.' And then I thought, 'Yes, that's all right. I'm poor and my clothes are cheap and perhaps it will always be like this. And that's all right too.' It was the first time in my life I'd thought that.

The ones without any money, the ones with beastly lives. Perhaps I'm going to be one of the ones with beastly lives. They swarm like woodlice when you push a stick into a woodlice-nest at home. And their faces are the colour of woodlice.

I felt ill when I woke up. I had pains all over me. I lay there and after a while I heard the landlady coming up the stairs. She was thin and younger than most landladies. She had black hair and little red eyes. I kept my head turned away so as not to see her.

'It's gone ten,' she said. 'I'm a bit late this morning with your breakfast but my clock stopped. This came for you; a messenger-boy brought it.'

There was a letter on the breakfast-tray, and a big bunch of violets. I took them up; they smelt like rain.

The landlady was watching me with her little red eyes. I said, 'Can I have my hot water?' and she went out.

I opened the letter and there were five five-pound notes inside.

'My dear Anna, I wish I could tell you how sweet you are. I'm worried about you. Will you buy yourself some stockings with this? And don't look anxious when you are buying them, please. Always yours, Walter Jeffries.'

When I heard the landlady coming back I put the money under my pillow. It crackled. She put the can of hot water down outside and went away.

The bunch of violets was too big for the tooth-glass. I put it in the water-jug.

I took the money from under my pillow and put it into

my handbag. I was accustomed to it already. It was as if I had always had it. Money ought to be everybody's. It ought to be like water. You can tell that because you get accustomed to it so quickly.

All the time I was dressing I was thinking what clothes I would buy. I didn't think of anything else at all, and I forgot about feeling ill.

Outside it smelt of melted snow.

The landlady was washing the steps. She plunged her hands into a pail of filthy water, wrung out the cloth and started to rub again. There she was on her knees.

'Will you lay a fire in my room, please?' I said. My voice sounded round and full instead of small and thin. 'That's because of the money,' I thought.

'You'll have to wait,' she said. 'I've got something else to do besides running up and down stairs laying fires.'

'I shan't be in again till this afternoon,' I said.

I looked back and she was kneeling upright staring after me. I thought, 'All right – stare.'

A dress and a hat and shoes and underclothes.

I got a taxi and told the driver to go to Cohen's in Shaftesbury Avenue.

There were two Miss Cohens and they really were sisters because their noses were the same and their eyes – opaque and shining – and their insolence that was only a mask. I knew the shop; I had been there with Laurie during rehearsals.

It was warm and it smelt of fur. There were two long mirrors and a sliding cupboard with the doors pushed back so that you could see the rows of dresses on hangers. The dresses, all colours, hanging there, waiting. The hats, except one or two on stands, were in a smaller room at the back.

The two Miss Cohens stared – one small and round, the other thin with a yellow face.

I said, 'Can I try on the dark blue dress and coat in the

window, please?' And the thin one advanced smiling. Her red lips smiled and her heavy lids drooped over her small, shiny eyes.

This is a beginning. Out of this warm room that smells of fur I'll go to all the lovely places I've ever dreamt of. This is the beginning.

The fat Miss Cohen went into the back room. I held my arms up and the thin one put on the dress as if I were a doll. The skirt was long and tight so that when I moved in it I saw the shape of my thighs.

'It's perfect,' she said. 'You could walk right out in it just as it is.'

I said, 'Yes, I like this. I'll keep it on.' But my face in the glass looked small and frightened.

The dress and coat cost eight guineas.

Then the other sister came in with a dark blue and white velvet cap. That cost two guineas.

When I took out the money to pay the thin Miss Cohen said, 'I have a very pretty little evening dress that would just suit you.' 'Not today,' I said. 'If you like the dress,' she said, 'you needn't pay at once.' I shook my head.

The fat one smiled and said, 'I remember you now. I thought I knew your face. Didn't you come in when Miss Gaynor was fitting her costume? Miss Laurie Gaynor?' 'That's right,' the thin one said, 'I remember. You were in the same company. How is Miss Gaynor?' The fat Miss Cohen said, 'We're having some new dresses in next week. Paris models. Come in and look at them and if you can't pay at once I daresay we can make an arrangement.'

The streets looked different that day, just as a reflection in the looking-glass is different from the real thing.

I went across the road to Jacobus and bought shoes. And then I bought underclothes and silk stockings. Then I had seven pounds left.

I began to feel ill again. When I breathed my side hurt. I got a taxi and went back to Judd Street.

The fire wasn't laid. I spread the underclothes I had bought on the bed and I was looking at them when the landlady came in with a scuttle of coals and sticks and paper.

I said, 'I'll be glad of the fire. I don't feel very well. Could you make me some tea?'

'You seem to think I'm here to wait on you,' she said.

When she had gone I got the letter out of my bag and read it through very carefully, sentence by sentence, to find out what each sentence meant. 'He doesn't say anything about seeing me again,' I thought.

'Here's your tea, Miss Morgan,' the landlady said. 'And I must ask you to find another room on Saturday. This room is reserved after Saturday.'

'Why didn't you tell me that when you let it to me?' I said.

She began to bawl. 'I don't hold with the way you go on, if you want to know, and my 'usband don't neither. Crawling up the stairs at three o'clock in the morning. And then today dressed up to the nines. I've got eyes in my head.'

'It wasn't three o'clock,' I said. 'What a lie!'

'I won't 'ave you calling me a liar,' she said. 'You and your drawly voice. And if you give me any of your lip I'll 'ave my 'usband up to you.'

At the door she turned round and said, 'I don't want no tarts in my house, so now you know.'

I didn't answer. My heart was beating like hell. I lay down and started thinking about the time when I was ill in Newcastle, and the room I had there, and that story about the walls of a room getting smaller and smaller until they crush you to death. *The Iron Shroud*, it was called. It wasn't Poe's story; it was more frightening than that. 'I believe this damned room's getting smaller and smaller,' I thought. And about the rows of houses outside, gimcrack, rotten-looking, and all exactly alike.

After a while I got a sheet of paper and wrote, 'Thank you for your letter. I've gone and got an awful cold. Would you come and see me, please? Would you come as soon as you get this? I mean if you care to. My landlady won't want to let you up, but she'll have to if you tell her that you're a relation and please do come.'

I went out and posted the letter and got some ammoniated quinine. It was nearly three o'clock. But when I had taken the quinine and had lain down again I felt too ill to care whether he came or not.

This is England, and I'm in a nice, clean English room with all the dirt swept under the bed.

It got dark, but I couldn't get up to light the gas. I felt as if there were weights on my legs so that I couldn't move. Like that time at home when I had fever and it was afternoon and the jalousies were down and yellow light came in through the slats and lay on the floor in bars. The room wasn't painted. There were knots in the wood and on one of them a cockroach, waving its feelers slowly backwards and forwards. I couldn't move. I lay watching it. I thought, 'If it flies on to the bed or if it flies on to my face I shall go mad.' I watched it and I thought, 'Is it going to fly?' and the bandage on my head was hot. Then Francine came in and she saw it and got a shoe and killed it. She changed the bandage round my head and it was ice-cold and she started fanning me with a palm-leaf fan. And then night outside and the voices of people passing in the street – the forlorn sound of voices, thin and sad. And the heat pressing down on you as if it were something alive. I wanted to be black. I always wanted to be black. I was happy because Francine was there, and I watched her hand waving the fan backwards and forwards and the beads of sweat that rolled from underneath her handkerchief. Being black is warm and gay, being white is cold and sad. She used to sing:

Adieu, sweetheart, adieu,
Salt beef and sardines too,
And all good times I leave behind,
Adieu, sweetheart, adieu.

That was her only English song.

– It was when I looked back from the boat and saw the
lights of the town bobbing up and down that was the first
time I really knew I was going. Uncle Bob said well
you're off now and I turned my head so that nobody
would see me crying – it ran down my face and splashed
into the sea like the rain was splashing – Adieu sweetheart adieu – And I watched the lights heaving up and
down –

He was standing in the doorway. I could see him
against the light in the passage.

'What's the time?' I said.

He said, 'It's half-past five. I came as soon as I got your
letter.'

He came up to the bed and put his hand on mine. He
said, 'But you're burning hot. You really are ill.'

'I should shay sho,' I said.

He took a box of matches out of his pocket and lit the
gas. 'My God, this isn't very cheerful.'

'It's like they all are,' I said.

The underclothes I had bought were heaped up on a
chair.

'I got a lot of clothes,' I said.

'Good.'

'And I've got to clear out of here.'

'That's a pretty good thing too, I should say,' he said.
'This really is an awful place.'

'It's so cold,' I said. 'That's the worst thing about it.
But where are you going?' Not that it mattered. I felt too
ill to care.

'I'll be back in ten minutes,' he said.

He came in again with a lot of parcels – an eiderdown and a bottle of burgundy and some grapes and Brand's essence of beef and a cold chicken.

He kissed me and his face felt cool and smooth against mine. But the heat and the cold of the fever were running up and down my back. When you have fever you are heavy and light, you are small and swollen, you climb endlessly a ladder which turns like a wheel.

I said, 'Take care. You'll catch my 'flu.'

'I expect I shall,' he said. 'It can't be helped.'

He sat down and smoked a cigarette, but I couldn't smoke. I liked watching him, though. It was as if I had always known him.

He said, 'Listen. Tomorrow I've got to go away, but I'll be back next week. I'm going to send my doctor in to see you tonight or tomorrow morning. Ames is his name. He's a nice chap, you'll like him. Just get well and don't worry, and write and tell me how you get on.'

'I've got to go out and look for another room to-morrow,' I said.

'Oh no,' he said. 'I'll speak to your landlady and I'll tell Ames to speak to her too. You'll find that'll be all right. Don't you worry about her.'

'I'd better take the food downstairs with me,' he said.

He went out. The room looked different, as if it had grown bigger.

After a while the landlady came in and put the opened bottle of wine and the soup on the table without speaking. I ate the soup, and then I drank two glasses of wine, and then I went to sleep.

3

There was a black table with curly legs in the hall in that house, and on it a square-faced clock, stopped at five minutes past twelve, and a plant made of rubber with shiny, bright red leaves, five-pointed. I couldn't take my eyes off it. It looked proud of itself, as if it knew that it was going on for ever and ever, as if it knew that it fitted in with the house and the street and the spiked iron railings outside.

The landlady came up from the kitchen.

'You'll be well enough to leave tomorrow, won't you, Miss Morgan?'

'Yes,' I said.

'That's all I wanted to know,' she said. But she stayed there staring at me, so I went outside and finished putting on my gloves standing on the doorstep. (A lady always puts on her gloves before going into the street.)

A man and a girl were leaning against the railings in Brunswick Square, kissing. They stood without moving in the shadow, with their mouths glued together. They were like beetles clinging to the railings.

·I got the glass out of my handbag and looked at myself every time the taxi passed a street-lamp. *It's soppy always to look sad. Funny stories – remember some, for God's sake.*

But the only story I could remember was the one about the curate. He laughed and then he said, 'You've got a hairpin sticking out on this side, spoiling your otherwise perfect appearance.'

When he pushed the hairpin back his hand touched my face and I tried to catch hold of myself and remember that the first time I had met him I hadn't liked him. But it seemed too long ago, so I stopped trying.

'Dr Ames was nice,' I said. 'He shut my landlady up like anything.'

I could still feel it on my face where his hand had touched me.

'Are you often ill like that in the winter?' he said. 'Last winter, yes,' I said. 'Not the first winter I was here. I was all right then; I didn't even think it very cold. They say it's always like that – it takes a year before the cold really gets you. But last winter I got pleurisy and the company had to leave me behind in Newcastle.' 'By yourself?' he said. 'How wretched!' 'Yes,' I said, 'it was. Three weeks I was there. It seemed like for ever.'

I didn't taste anything I ate. The orchestra played Puccini and the sort of music that you always know what's going to come next, that you can listen to ahead, as it were; and I could still feel it on my face where his hand had touched me. I kept trying to imagine his life.

When we went out the taxis and the lights and the people passing looked swollen, as if I were drunk. We got to his house in Green Street and it was quiet and watching and not friendly to me.

'I was expecting to have a letter from you all last week,' he said, 'and you never wrote. Why didn't you?'

'I wanted to see if you would,' I said.

The sofa was soft and fat, covered in chintz with a pattern of small blue flowers. He put his hand on my knee and I thought, 'Yes ... yes ... yes. ...' Sometimes it's like that – everything drops away except the one moment.

'When I sent you that money I never meant – I never thought I should see you again,' he said.

'I know, but I wanted to see you again,' I said.

Then he started talking about my being a virgin and it all went – the feeling of being on fire – and I was cold.

'Why did you start about that?' I said. 'What's it

matter? Besides, I'm not a virgin if that's what's worrying you.'

'You oughtn't to tell lies about that.'

'I'm not telling lies, but it doesn't matter, anyway,' I said. 'People have made all that up.'

'Oh yes, it matters. It's the only thing that matters.'

'It's not the only thing that matters,' I said. 'All that's made up.'

He stared at me and then he laughed. 'You're quite right,' he said.

But I felt cold, as if someone had thrown cold water over me. When he kissed me I began to cry.

'I must go,' I thought. 'Where's the door? I can't see the door. What's happened?' It was as if I were blind.

He wiped my eyes very gently with his handkerchief, but I kept saying, 'I must go, I must go.' Then we were going up another flight of stairs and I walked softly. *'Crawling up the stairs at three o'clock in the morning,' she said. Well, I'm crawling up the stairs.*

I stopped. I wanted to say, 'No, I've changed my mind.' But he laughed and squeezed my hand and said, 'What's the matter? Come on, be brave,' and I didn't say anything, but I felt cold and as if I were dreaming.

When I got into bed there was warmth coming from him and I got close to him. *Of course you've always known, always remembered, and then you forget so utterly, except that you've always known it. Always – how long is always?*

The things spread out on the dressing-table shone in the light of the fire, and I thought, 'When I shut my eyes I'll be able to see this room all my life.'

I said, 'I must go now. What's the time?'

'It's half-past three,' he said.

'I must go,' I said again, whispering.

He said, 'You mustn't be sad, you mustn't worry. My darling mustn't be sad.'

I lay quite still, thinking, 'Say it again. Say "darling" again like that. Say it again.'

But he didn't speak and I said, 'I'm not sad. Why have you got this soppy idea that I'm always sad?'

I got up and started to dress. The ribbons in my chemise looked silly.

'I don't like your looking-glass,' I said.

'Don't you?' he said.

'Have you ever noticed how different some looking-glasses make you look?' I said.

I went on dressing without looking at myself again in the glass. I thought that it had been just like the girls said, except that I hadn't known it would hurt so much.

'Can I have a drink?' I said. 'I'm awfully thirsty.'

He said, 'Yes, have some more wine. Or would you like something else?'

'I'd like a whisky-and-soda,' I said.

There was a tray with drinks on the table. He poured one out for me.

He said. 'Now, wait a bit. I'll come with you to get a taxi.'

There was a telephone over by the bed. I thought, 'Why doesn't he telephone for a taxi?' but I didn't say anything.

He went into the bathroom. I was still very thirsty. I filled the glass up again with soda-water and drank it in small sips, not thinking of anything. It was as if everything in my head had stopped.

He came into the room again and I watched him in the glass. My handbag was on the table. He took it up and put some money into it. Before he did it he looked towards me but he thought I couldn't see him. I got up. I meant to say, 'What are you doing?' But when I went up to him instead of saying, 'Don't do that,' I said. 'All right, if you like – anything you like, any way you like.' And I kissed his hand.

'Don't,' he said. 'It's I who ought to kiss your hand, not you mine.'

I felt miserable suddenly and utterly lost. 'Why did I do that?' I thought.

But as soon as we were out in the street I felt happy again, and calm and peaceful. We walked along in the fog and he was holding my hand.

I could feel the pulse in his wrist.

We got a taxi in Park Lane.

'Well, good-bye,' I said.

He said, 'I'll write to you tomorrow.'

'Will you write to me so that I get it early?' I said.

'Yes, I'll send it by messenger. You'll get it when you wake up.'

'You've got my new address, haven't you? You won't go and lose it.'

'Yes, yes, I've got it,' he said. 'I won't lose it.'

'I'm awfully sleepy,' I said. 'I bet I'll go to sleep in this taxi.'

When I paid the man he winked at me. I looked over his head and pretended not to notice.

4

My new rooms were in Adelaide Road, not far from Chalk Farm Tube station. There wasn't anything much to do all day. I would get up late and then go out for a walk and then go back home and have something to eat and watch out of the window for a telegraph-boy or a messenger. Every time the postman knocked I would think, 'Is that a letter for me?'

There was always some old man trailing along singing

hymns – 'Nearer, my God, to Thee' or 'Abide with me' –
and people making up their minds ten yards off that they
were not going to see them and others not seeing them
at all. Invisible men, they were. But the oldest one of
all played 'The Girl I Left Behind Me' on a penny
whistle.

There was a moulding round the walls of the sitting-
room – grapes, pineapples and acanthus leaves, all very
dirty. The light in the middle hung from more acanthus
leaves. It was a large, square room, high-ceilinged, with
four chairs placed against the walls, a piano, a sofa, one
armchair and a table in the middle. It reminded me of a
restaurant, that's why I liked it.

I would think about when he made love to me and walk
up and down thinking about it; and that I hated the
looking-glass in his room – it made me look so thin and
pale. And about getting up and saying, 'I must go now,'
and dressing, and going down the stairs quietly, and the
front door that clicked so silently, that clicked always as
if it were for the last time, and there I was in the dark
street.

Of course, you get used to things, you get used to anything. It was as if I had always lived like that. Only sometimes, when I had got back home and was undressing to
go to bed, I would think, 'My God, this is a funny way to
live. My God, how did this happen?'

Sunday was the worst day, because he was never in
London and there wasn't any hope that he would send for
me. That year my birthday was on a Sunday. The seventh
of January. I was nineteen. The night before he sent me
roses and said in his letter: 'Nineteen is a great age. How
old do you think I am? Never mind. Tottering, I expect
you would say if you knew.' And he said that he wanted
me to meet his cousin Vincent at dinner on Monday, and
that he'd thought of a present I'd like. 'I think I'll tell
you about that.'

There had been a card from Maudie: 'Coming to see you Sunday afternoon. Cheerio. Maudie.'

I lay in bed pretty late because there wasn't anything else to do. When I got up I went out for a walk. It's funny how parts of London are as empty as if they were dead. There was no sun, but there was a glare on everything like a brass band playing.

In the afternoon it began to rain. I lay down on the sofa and tried to sleep, but I couldn't because a church bell started with that tinny, nagging sound they have. The feeling of Sunday is the same everywhere, heavy, melancholy, standing still. Like when they say, 'As it was in the beginning, is now, and ever shall be, world without end.'

I thought about home and standing by the window on Sunday morning, dressing to go to church, and putting on a woollen vest which had shrunk in the wash and was too small, because wool next the skin is healthy. And white drawers tight at the knee and a white petticoat and a white embroidered dress – everything starched and prickly. And black ribbed-wool stockings with black shoes. (The groom Joseph cleaning the shoes with blacking and spit. Spit – mix – rub; spit – mix – rub. Joseph had heaps of spittle and when he spurted a jet into the tin of blacking he never missed.) And brown kid gloves straight from England, one size too small. 'Oh, you naughty girl, you're trying to split those gloves; you're trying to split those gloves on purpose.'

(While you are carefully putting on your gloves you begin to perspire and you feel the perspiration trickling down under your arms. The thought of having a wet patch underneath your arms – a disgusting and a disgraceful thing to happen to a lady – makes you very miserable.)

And the sky close to the earth. Hard, blue and close to the earth. The mangotree was so big that all the garden was in its shadow and the ground under it always looked dark and damp. The stable-yard was by the side of the garden, white-paved and hot, smelling of horses and manure. And then next to the stables was a bathroom. And the bathroom too was always dark and damp. It had no windows, but the door used to be hooked a little bit open. The light was always dim, greenish. There were cobwebs on the roof.

The stone bath was half as big as a good-sized room. You went up into it by two stone steps, cool and lovely to your feet. Then you sat on the side of the bath and let your legs dangle into the dark green water.

'"... And all the Roy-al Fam-i-lee."

'"We beseech thee to hear us, good Lord." '

During the Litany I would bite the back of the pitch-pine pew in front, and sigh, and read bits of the marriage-service, and fan myself with an old wire fan with a picture on it in faded blues and reds of a fat Chinese woman toppling over backwards. Her little fat feet, with slippers turned up at the toes, seemed to be moving in the air; her little fat hands clutched at nothingness.

'To the Memory of Doctor Charles Le Mesurier, the Poor of this Island were Grateful for his Benevolence, the Rich Rewarded his Industry and Skill.' That gave you a peaceful and melancholy feeling. The poor do this and the rich do that, the world is so-and-so and nothing can change it. For ever and for ever turning and nothing, nothing can change it.

Red, blue, green, purple in the stained-glass windows. And saints with bare, wax-coloured feet with long, supple toes.

'"We beseech thee to hear us, good Lord." '

Always, just when I had fallen into a sort of stupor, the Litany would end.

Walking through the still palms in the churchyard.

The light is gold and when you shut your eyes you see fire-colour.

'What have you done to yourself?' Maudie said. 'You look different. I'd have been round to see you before, but I've been away. You've done something to your hair, haven't you? It's lighter.' I said, 'Yes, I've had henna-shampoos. Do you like it?' 'In a way I do,' Maudie said. 'It's not bad.'

She sat down and began a long discourse. Every now and then she would giggle a nervous and meaningless giggle. When I remember living with her it was like looking at an old photograph of myself and thinking, 'What on earth's that got to do with me?'

I had some vermouth. I got it out and we each had a drink.

'It's my birthday. Wish me many happy returns.'

'You bet I do,' Maudie said. 'Here's to us. Who's like us? Damned few. What a life!'

'You've got swanky rooms, anyway,' she said. 'A piano and everything.' 'Yes, they're all right,' I said. 'Have another.' 'Ta,' Maudie said.

When I had finished the second vermouth I felt I wanted to tell her about it.

'What, the man you got off with at Southsea?' Maudie said. 'He's got a lot of money, hasn't he? D'you know, I always knew you'd get off with somebody with money. I was saying so only the other day. I said, "It's all very well, but I bet you she gets off with somebody with money."'

'What did I talk about it for?' I thought.

'I don't know what I'm laughing at,' Maudie said. 'It's nothing to laugh about really. I like this drink. Can I have some more?'

'Only, don't get soppy about him,' she said. 'That's fatal. The thing with men is to get everything you can out of them and not care a damn. You ask any girl in London – or any girl in the whole world if it comes to that – who really knows, and she'll tell you the same thing.' 'I've heard all that a million times,' I said. 'I'm sick of hearing it.' 'Oh, I needn't talk,' Maudie said, 'the fool I made myself over Viv! Though it was a bit different with me, you understand. We were going to be married.'

'What a life!' she said.

We went into the bedroom. 'Cherry Ripe' over the washstand and facing it another picture of a little girl in a white dress with a blue sash fondling a woolly dog.

Maudie stared at the bed, which was small and narrow.

'He never comes here,' I said. 'We go to his house or different places. He's never been here at all.' 'Oh, that's the sort he is,' Maudie said, 'the cautious sort, is he? Viv was awfully cautious too. It's not such a good sign when they're like that.'

Then she started telling me that I ought to swank as much as I could.

'I don't want to interfere, kid, but really you ought. The more you swank the better. If you don't swank a bit nothing's any use. If he's a rich man and he's keeping you, you ought to make him get you a nice flat up West somewhere and furnish it for you. Then you'd have something. I remember – he said he worked in the City. Is he one of these Stock Exchange blokes?' 'Yes,' I said, 'but he's something to do with an insurance company too. I don't know; he doesn't talk much about himself.' 'There you are – the cautious sort,' Maudie said.

She looked at my dresses and kept saying, 'Very lady-like. I call that one very ladylike indeed. And you've got a fur coat. Well, if a girl has a lot of good clothes and a fur coat she has something, there's no getting away from that.'

'My dear, I had to laugh,' she said. 'D'you know what a

man said to me the other day? It's funny, he said, have you ever thought that a girl's clothes cost more than the girl inside them?'

'What a swine of a man!' I said.

'Yes, that's what I told him,' Maudie said. '"That isn't the way to talk," I said. And he said, "Well, it's true, isn't it? You can get a very nice girl for five pounds, a very nice girl indeed; you can even get a very nice girl for nothing if you know how to go about it. But you can't get a very nice costume for her for five pounds. To say nothing of underclothes, shoes, etcetera and so on." And then I had to laugh, because after all it's true, isn't it? People are much cheaper than things. And look here! Some dogs are more expensive than people, aren't they? And as to some horses ...'

'Oh, shut up,' I said. 'You're getting on my nerves. Let's go back into the sitting-room; it's cold in here.'

'What about your stepmother?' Maudie said. 'What'll she think if you chuck the tour? Are you going to chuck it?' 'I don't know what she'll think,' I said. 'I don't suppose she'll think anything.' 'Well, I call that funny,' Maudie said. 'I will say that for your stepmother. She doesn't seem to be at all inquisitive, does she?' 'I shall tell her that I'm trying for a job in London. Why should she think it funny?' I said.

Looking out at the street was like looking at stagnant water. Hester was coming up to London in February. I started wondering what I should say to her, and I began to feel depressed. I said, 'I don't like London. It's an awful place; it looks horrible sometimes. I wish I'd never come over here at all.'

'You must be potty,' Maudie said. 'Whoever heard of anybody who didn't like London?' Her eyes looked scornful.

'Well, everybody doesn't,' I said. 'You listen to this thing.' I got it out of the drawer and read:

'Horse faces, faces like horses,
And grey streets, where old men wail unnoticed
Prayers to an ignoble God.
There the butcher's shop stinks to the leaden sky;
There the fish shop stinks differently, but worse.

And so on, and so on.'
Then there were a lot of dots. And then it went on:

'But where are they –
The cool arms, white as alabaster?'

'Well,' Maudie said, 'what's all that about?'
'Just listen to this one,' I said:

'Loathsome London, vile and stinking hole . . .'

'Hey,' Maudie said, 'that's enough of that.'
I began to laugh. I said, 'That's the man who had these rooms before me. The landlady told me about him. She had to chuck him out because he couldn't pay his rent. I found these things in a drawer.'

'He must have been up the pole,' Maudie said. 'D'you know, I thought there was something about this place that gave me the pip; I'm awfully sensitive like that. Anybody funny around – I always feel it in a minute. And besides, I hate high ceilings. And those blasted pineapples round the walls. It isn't cosy.'

'You ought to make him give you a flat,' she said. 'Park Mansions, that's the place. I bet he's fond of you and he will. But don't go and wait too long before you ask him, because that's fatal too.'

'Well, if we're going out,' I said, 'we'd better go. It'll be pitch-dark in a minute.'

We took the Tube to Marble Arch, and walked through the Park. Some distance away from the crowd round the speakers, there was a man standing on a box, bawling something about God. Nobody was listening to him. You could only hear 'God. . . . God. . . . The wrath of God. . . . Wah, wah, wah, wah . . .'

We got up close to him. I could see the Adam's apple jumping up and down in his throat. Maudie began to laugh, and he got wild and shrieked after us, 'Laugh! Your sins will find you out. Already the fear of death and hell is in your hearts, already the fear of God is like fire in your hearts.'

'Well, the dirty tyke!' Maudie said. 'Insulting us just because we haven't got a man with us. I know these people, they're careful who they're rude to. They're damned careful who they try to convert. Have you ever noticed? He wouldn't have said a word if we'd had a man with us.'

We heard his voice after us, *God*, wah, wah, wah. . . . *God*, wah, wah, wah . . .'

He was thin and he looked cold. He had little, sad eyes. But Maudie was very vexed. She walked faster than usual, swinging her arms and saying, 'Dirty little tyke, dirty little tyke. . . . They're damned careful who they try to convert.'

But I wanted to go back and talk to him and find out what he was really thinking of, because his eyes had a blind look, like a dog's when it sniffs something.

We took a bus at Hyde Park Corner and went to a place that Maudie knew of near Victoria Station. We had oysters and stout.

Maudie got a bus to go home.

'Well,' she said, 'look here, do write to me, kid. Let me know what happens. Take care of yourself and if you can't be good be careful. Etcetera and so on.'

I said, 'Don't be surprised if I turn up at rehearsals.'

'Oh no, I won't be surprised,' she said. 'I've given up being surprised.'

5

Next evening, we got back to Green Street about eleven o'clock. There was the light on over the sofa and the tray with drinks, and the rest of the house dark and quiet and not friendly to me. Sneering faintly, sneering discreetly, as a servant would. Who's this? Where on earth did he pick her up?

'Well,' he said, 'what did you think of Vincent? He's a good-looking boy, isn't he?'

'Yes,' I said, 'very.'

'He likes you. He thinks you're a darling.'

'Oh, does he? I thought he didn't, somehow.'

'Good Lord, why?'

'I don't know,' I said. 'I just thought so.'

'Of course he likes you. He says he wants to hear you sing some time.'

'What for?' I said.

It was raining hard. When I listened I could just hear the sound of it.

'Because he could probably do something about getting you a job. He's very much in with some of these people and he might be most awfully useful to you. As a matter of fact he offered to do what he could for you off his own bat; I didn't ask him.'

'Well, I could go back on tour if it comes to that,' I said.

I was thinking about when he would start kissing me and about when we would go upstairs.

'We're going to get you something much better than that. Vincent says he doesn't see why you shouldn't get on, and I don't see why you shouldn't either. I believe it would be a good idea for you to have singing-lessons. I want to help you; I want you to get on. You want to get on, don't you?'

'I don't know,' I said.

'But, my dear, how do you mean you don't know? Good God, you must know. What would you really like to do?'

I said, 'I want to be with you. That's all I want.'

'Oh, you'll soon get sick of me.' He smiled, a bit as if he were sneering at me.

I didn't answer.

'Don't be like that,' he said. 'Don't be like a stone that I try to roll uphill and that always rolls down again.'

'Like a stone,' he said. It's funny how you think, 'It won't hurt until I move.' So you sit perfectly still. Even your face goes stiff.

He was saying, 'You're a perfect darling, but you're only a baby. You'll be all right later on. Not that it has anything to do with age. Some people are born knowing their way about; others never learn. Your predecessor –'

'My predecessor?' I said. 'Oh! my predecessor.'

'She was certainly born knowing her way about. It doesn't matter, though. Don't worry. Do believe me, you haven't got to worry.'

'Yes, of course,' I said.

'Well, look happy then. Be happy. I want you to be happy.'

'All right, I'll have a whisky,' I said. 'No, not wine – whisky.'

'You've learnt to like whisky already, haven't you?' he said.

'It's in my blood,' I said. 'All my family drink too much. You should see my Uncle Ramsay – Uncle Bo. He can drink if you like.'

'That's all very fine and large,' Walter said, 'but don't start too early.'

... Here's the punch Uncle Bo said welcome Hebe – this child certainly can mix a good punch Father said something to warm the cockles of your heart – the blinds on the verandah were flapping – like a sip Father said whoa he said that'll do we don't want to have you starting too early ...

'Yes, Uncle Bo can drink if you like,' I said, 'and you wouldn't think so; it never seems to make any difference to him. He's nice. I like him much better than my other uncle.'

'You're a rum little devil, aren t you?' Walter said.

'Oh, I always was rum,' I said. 'When I was a kid I wanted to be black, and they used to say, "Your poor grandfather would turn in his grave if he heard you talking like that." '

I finished the whisky. The paralysed feeling went and I was all right again. 'Oh well,' I thought, 'I don't care. What's it matter?'

'I'm the fifth generation born out there, on my mother's side.'

'Are you really?' he said, still a bit as if he were laughing at me.

'I wish you could see Constance Estate,' I said. 'That's the old estate – my mother's family place. It's very beautiful. I wish you could see it.'

'I wish I could,' he said. 'I'm sure it's beautiful.'

'Yes,' I said. 'On the other hand, if England is beautiful, it's not beautiful. It's some other world. It all depends, doesn't it?'

Thinking of the walls of the Old Estate house, still standing, with moss on them. That was the garden. One ruined room for roses, one for orchids, one for tree ferns. And the honeysuckle all along the steep flight of steps that led down to the room where the overseer kept his books.

'I saw an old slave-list at Constance once,' I said. 'It was hand-written on that paper that rolls up. Parchment, d'you call it? It was in columns – the names and the ages and what they did and then General Remarks.'

... Maillotte Boyd, aged 18, mulatto, house servant. The sins of the fathers Hester said are visited upon the children unto the third and fourth generation – don't talk such nonsense to the child Father said – a myth don't get tangled up in myths he said to me ...

'All those names written down,' I said. 'It's funny, I've never forgotten it.'

I suppose it was the whisky, but I wanted to talk about it. I wanted to make him see what it was like. And it all went through my head, but too quickly. Besides, you can never tell about things.

'There was a girl at school,' I said, 'at the convent I went to. Beatrice Agostini, her name was. She came from Venezuela, she was a boarder. I liked her awfully. I wasn't a boarder, of course, except once when my father went to England for six months. When he came back he had married again; he brought Hester with him.'

'Your stepmother was all right to you, wasn't she?'

'Yes, she was all right. She was very nice – in a way.'

'We used to go for moonlight rows,' I said. 'Black Pappy was our boatman's name. We have lovely moonlight nights. You should see them. The shadows the moon makes are as dark as sun-shadows.'

Black Pappy used to wear a blue linen suit, the trousers patched behind with sacking. He had very long ears and a round gold earring in one of them. He would bawl out at you that you mustn't trail your hand in the water on account of the barracoutas. Then you would imagine the barracoutas – hundreds of them – swimming by the side of the boat, waiting to snap. Flat-headed, sharp-toothed, swimming along the cold white roads the moon makes on the water.

'I'm sure it's beautiful,' Walter said, 'but I don't like hot places much. I prefer cold places. The tropics would be altogether too lush for me, I think.'

'But it isn't lush,' I said. 'You're quite wrong. It's

wild, and a bit sad sometimes. You might as well say the sun's lush.'

Sometimes the earth trembles; sometimes you can feel it breathe. The colours are red, purple, blue, gold, all shades of green. The colours here are black, brown, grey, dim-green, pale blue, the white of people's faces – like woodlice.

'Besides, it wasn't as hot as all that,' I said. 'They exaggerate about the heat. It got a bit hot in the town sometimes, but my father had a little estate called Morgan's Rest, and we were there a lot. He was a planter, my father. He had a big estate when he first went out there; then he sold it when he married Hester and we lived in the town for nearly four years and then he bought Morgan's Rest – a much smaller place. He called it that, Morgan's Rest.'

'My father was a fine man,' I said, feeling rather drunk. 'He had a red moustache and he had a most terrible temper. Not as bad as Mr Crowe's, though Mr Crowe had been out there forty years and he had such a terrible temper that one day he bit his pipe right in two – or that's what the servants said. And whenever he was at home I used to watch him and hope he'd do it again, but he never did.'

'I disliked my father,' Walter said. 'I thought most people did.'

'Oh, I didn't mine,' I said. 'Not all the time anyway.'

'I'm a real West Indian,' I kept saying. 'I'm the fifth generation on my mother's side.'

'I know, my sweet,' Walter said. 'You told me that before.'

'I don't care,' I said. 'It was a lovely place.'

'Everybody thinks the place where he was born is lovely,' Walter said.

'Well, they aren't all lovely,' I said. 'Not by a long chalk. In fact, some of them give you a shock at first, they're so ugly. Only you get used to it; you don't notice it after a while.'

He got up and pulled me up and started kissing me.

'You sound a bit tight,' he said. 'Well, let's go upstairs, you rum child, you rum little devil.'

'Champagne and whisky is a great mixture,' he said. We went upstairs.

'Children, every day one should put aside a quarter of an hour for meditation on the Four Last Things. Every night before going to sleep – that's the best time – you should shut your eyes and try to think of one of the Four Last Things.' (*Question*: What are the Four Last Things? *Answer*: The Four Last Things are Death, Judgement, Hell and Heaven.) That was Mother St Anthony – funny old thing she was, too. She would say, 'Children, every night before you go to sleep you should lie straight down with your arms by your sides and your eyes shut and say: "One day I shall be dead. One day I shall lie like this with my eyes closed and I shall be dead."' 'Are you afraid of dying?' Beatrice would say. 'No, I don't believe I am. Are you?' 'Yes, I am, but I never think about it.'

Lying down with your arms by your sides and your eyes shut.

'Walter, will you put the light out? I don't like it in my eyes.'

Maillotte Boyd, aged 18. *Maillotte Boyd, aged* 18. ... *But I like it like this. I don't want it any other way but this.*

'Are you asleep?'

'No, I'm not asleep.'

'You were lying so still,' he said.

Lying so still afterwards. That's what they call the Little Death.

'I must go now,' I said. 'It's getting late.'

I got up and dressed.

'I'll arrange about Vincent,' he said. 'Some afternoon next week.'

'All right,' I said.

All the way back in the taxi I was still thinking about home and when I got into bed I lay awake, thinking about it. About how sad the sun can be, especially in the afternoon, but in a different way from the sadness of cold places, quite different. And the way the bats fly out at sunset, two by two, very stately. And the smell of the store down on the Bay. ('I'll take four yards of the pink, please, Miss Jessie.') And the smell of Francine – acrid-sweet. And that hibiscus once – it was so red, so proud, and its long gold tongue hung out. It was so red that even the sky was just a background for it. And I can't believe it's dead. ... And the sound of rain on the galvanized-iron roof. How it would go on and on, thundering on the roof ...

That was when it was sad, when you lay awake at night and remembered things. That was when it was sad, when you stood by the bed and undressed, thinking, 'When he kisses me, shivers run up my back. I am hopeless, resigned, utterly happy. Is that me? I am bad, not good any longer, bad. That has no meaning, absolutely none. Just words. But something about the darkness of the streets has a meaning.'

6

Hester usually came up to London for the January sales, but it was the middle of March before she wrote to me from a boarding-house in Bayswater.

'Yes, Mrs Morgan's expecting you,' the maid said. 'She's at lunch.'

'I'm sorry I'm late,' I said, and Hester said, 'I'm glad to see you looking so well.'

She had clear brown eyes which stuck out of her head if you looked at her sideways, and an English lady's voice with a sharp, cutting edge to it. Now that I've spoken you can hear that I'm a lady. I have spoken and I suppose you now realize that I'm an English gentlewoman. I have my doubts about you. Speak up and I will place you at once. Speak up, for I fear the worst. That sort of voice.

There were two middle-aged women at our table and a young man with a newspaper which he read whenever he stopped eating. The stew tasted of nothing at all. Everybody took one mouthful and then showered salt and sauce out of a bottle on to it. Everybody did this mechanically, without a change of expression, so that you saw they knew it would taste of nothing. If it had tasted of anything they would have suspected it.

There was an advertisement at the back of the newspaper: 'What is Purity? For Thirty-five Years the Answer has been Bourne's Cocoa.'

'I've got a letter here that I want to read to you,' Hester said. 'It came just before I left Ilkley. I'm rather upset about it.'

'But not here,' she said. 'Upstairs, later on.' Then she said that the rector's daughter was getting married and that she was going to give her a present of two jumbie-beads set in gold and made into a brooch.

'The niggers say that jumbie-beads are lucky, don't they?'

'Yes, they do,' I said. 'They always say that.'

We ate tinned pears and then she said, 'Well, now we'll go to my room, I think.'

'This is the brooch,' she said, when we got upstairs. 'Don't you think it's charming?'

'Awfully pretty,' I said.

She put it back into its box and began to stroke her

upper lip, as if she had an invisible moustache. She had a habit of doing that. Her hands were large with broad palms, but the fingers were long and slender and she was proud of them.

'You really are looking astonishingly well,' she said. 'What about your new engagement? Have you started rehearsing yet?'

'Well, not just yet,' I said.

She blinked and went on stroking her upper lip.

'Perhaps I'll be in a London show starting in September,' I said. 'I'm having singing-lessons now. I began them three weeks ago. With a man called Price. He's very good.'

'Really?' she said, lifting her eyebrows.

I sat there. I didn't know what to say. There wasn't anything to say. I kept on wondering whether she would ask me what I was living on. 'What is Purity? For Thirty-five Years the Answer has been Bourne's Cocoa.' Thirty-five years. ... Fancy being thirty-five years old. What is Purity? For Thirty-five Thousand Years the Answer has been ...

She cleared her throat. She said, 'This letter is from your Uncle Ramsay. It's in answer to one I wrote about you two months ago.'

'About me?' I said.

She said, without looking at me, 'I wrote suggesting that you should go home again. I told him that things didn't seem to be turning out as I had hoped when I brought you over here, and that I was worried about you, and that I thought this might be the best thing.'

'Oh, I see,' I said.

'Well, I *am* worried about you,' she said. 'I was shocked when I saw you after your illness in Newcastle last winter. Besides ... I feel it's altogether too much responsibility for me.'

'And that's what Uncle Bo wrote back, is it?' I said.

'Uncle Bo!' she said. 'Uncle Bo! Uncle Boozy would be a better name for him. Yes, this is what Uncle Bo wrote back.'

She put her glasses on.

She said, 'Listen to this: "As a matter of fact I wanted to write to you about Anna some time ago when she started trapesing about the place pretending to be a chorus-girl or whatever you call it. Then I thought that as you were on the spot you were perhaps the best judge of what it was suitable for her to do. So I didn't interfere. Now you write this extraordinary letter telling me that you don't think life in England is agreeing with her very well and that you are willing to pay half her passage out here. Half her passage. But where's the other half coming from? That's what I should like to know. It's a bit late in the day for plain speaking, but better late than never. You know as well as I do that the responsibility for Anna's support is yours and I won't tolerate for a minute any attempt to shift it on to my shoulders. Poor Gerald spent the last of his capital on Morgan's Rest (much against my advice, I may say) and he meant it eventually to be his daughter's property. But, as soon as he was dead, you chose to sell the place and leave the island. You had perfect right to sell it; he left it to you. He had every faith and confidence in you, otherwise his will might have been different. Poor chap. So when you write and propose paying 'half her passage money' and sending her back out here without a penny in her pocket I can only answer that it seems to me there must be some misunderstanding, that you can't be serious. If you feel that you don't wish her to live with you in England, of course her aunt and I will have her here with us. But in that case I insist – we both insist – that she should have her proper share of the money you got from the sale of her father's estate. Anything else would be iniquitous – iniquitous is the only word. You know as well as I do that there is not the remotest chance of her ever being able to earn any money for herself out here. This is a most unpleasant letter to have to write and I can only end by saying that I am sorry it had to be written. I hope you are both well. We hardly ever hear from Anna. She's a strange child. She sent us a postcard from Blackpool or some such town and all she said on it was, 'This is a very windy place,' which doesn't tell us much about how she is getting on. Tell her from me to be a sensible girl and try to settle down. Though I must say that to give a girl the idea you're trying to get rid of her is hardly the way to make her settle down. Her Aunt Sase sends her love." '

'That's an outrageous letter,' Hester said.

She began to tap on the table.

'That letter,' she said, 'was written with one solitary aim and object – it was written to hurt and grieve me. It's an outrageous thing to accuse me of cheating you out of your father's money. I got five hundred pounds for Morgan's Rest, that was all. Five hundred. And your father bamboozled into paying eight hundred and fifty. But that had nothing to do with me on the contrary if I could have stopped him I would have done so and your famous Uncle Bo had a finger in that pie too whatever he says now. The way English people are cheated into buying estates that aren't worth a halfpenny is a shame. Estate! Fancy calling a place like that an estate. Only I must say that your father ought to have known better after thirty years out there and losing touch with everybody in England. Once he said to me, "No, I never want to go back. It cost me too much last time and I didn't really enjoy it. I've got nobody there who cares a damn about me. The place stinks of hypocrites if you've got a nose," he said. "I don't care if I never see it again." When he said that I knew he was failing. And such a brilliant man poor man buried alive you might say yes it was a tragedy a tragedy. But still he ought to have known better than to have let himself be cheated in the way he was cheated first and last. Morgan's Rest! Call it Morgan's Folly I told him and you won't be far wrong. Sell it! I should think I did sell a place that lost money and always has done and always will do every penny of money that anybody is stupid enough to put into it and nothing but rocks and stones and heat and those awful doves cooing all the time. And never seeing a white face from one week's end to the other and you growing up more like a nigger every day. Enough to drive anybody mad. I should think I did sell it. And that overseer man pretending that he couldn't speak English and getting ready to rob me right and left ...'

I had been expecting something so different that what she was saying didn't seem to make any sense. I was looking out of the window. The leaves of the trees in the square were coming out, and there was a pigeon strutting in the street with its neck all green and gold.

'And then I had to pay your father's debts,' she said. 'When I left the island I left with under three hundred in my pocket and out of that I paid your passage to England I fitted you out to go to school you hadn't a garment that was suitable for the winter a complete outfit – everything – had to be bought and I bore your expenses for a term. And when I wrote and asked your uncle to help to keep you at school for a year because you ought to have some sort of decent education if you were going to earn your living and a term wasn't long enough to make any impression or do any real good he said he couldn't afford it because he had three children of his own to support. He sent five pounds to buy a warm dress because if he remembered England rightly you'd be shivering. And I thought three children what about the others you horrible old man what about the others all colours of the rainbow. And my income is under three hundred a year and that's *my* income and out of that last year I sent you at one time and another thirty pounds and I paid your expenses and your doctor's bill when you were ill in Newcastle and that time you had a tooth stopped I paid that too. I can't afford to give you nearly fifty pounds a year. And all the thanks I get is this outrageous charge that I've cheated you and all the responsibility for the way you're going on must be put on my shoulders. Because don't imagine that I don't guess how you're going on. Only some things must be ignored some things I refuse to be mixed up with I refuse to think about even. And your mother's family stand aside and do nothing. I shall write once more to your uncle and after that I shall have no further communication with your mother's family whatever. They always disliked me,' she said, 'and they didn't trouble to conceal it but this letter is the last straw.'

She had started talking slowly, but it now seemed as if she couldn't stop. Her face was red. 'Like a rushing river, that woman,' as Uncle Bo used to say.

'Oh, I don't suppose he meant anything,' I said. 'He's one of those people who always says much more than he means instead of the other way about.'

She said, 'I shall mean every word of the answer I send. Your uncle is not a gentleman and I shall tell him so.'

'Oh, he won't mind that,' I said. I couldn't help laughing. Thinking of Uncle Bo getting a letter which began 'Dear Ramsay, You are not a gentleman . . .'

'I'm glad you see it's laughable,' she said. 'A gentleman! With illegitimate children wandering about all over the place called by his name – called by his name if you please. Sholto Costerus, Mildred Costerus, Dagmar. The Costeruses seem to have populated half the island in their time it's too funny. And you being told they were your cousins and giving them presents every Christmas and your father had got so slack that he said he didn't see any harm in it. He was a tragedy your father yes a tragedy and such a brilliant man poor man. But I gave Ramsay a piece of my mind one day I spoke out I said, "My idea of a gentleman an English gentleman doesn't have illegitimate children and if he does he doesn't flaunt them." "No I bet he doesn't," he said, laughing in that greasy way – exactly the laugh of a Negro he had – "I should think being flaunted is the last thing that happens to the poor little devils. Not much flaunting of that sort done in England." Horrible man! How I always disliked him! ...'

'Unfortunate propensities,' she said. 'Unfortunate propensities which were obvious to me from the first. But considering everything you probably can't help them. I always pitied you. I always thought that considering everything you were much to be pitied.'

I said, 'How do you mean, "considering everything"?'

'You know exactly what I mean, so don't pretend.'

'You're trying to make out that my mother was coloured,' I said. 'You always did try to make that out. And she wasn't.'

'I'm trying to make out nothing of the kind. You say unforgivable things sometimes – wicked and unforgivable things.'

I said, 'Well, what did you mean then?'

'I'm not going to argue with you,' she said. 'My conscience is quite clear. I always did my best for you and I never got any thanks for it. I tried to teach you to talk like a lady and behave like a lady and not like a nigger and of course I couldn't do it. Impossible to get you away from the servants. That awful sing-song voice you had! Exactly like a nigger you talked – and still do. Exactly like that dreadful girl Francine. When you were jabbering away together in the pantry I never could tell which of you was speaking. But I did think when I brought you to England that I was giving you a real chance. And now that you're beginning to turn out badly I must be made responsible for it and I must go on supporting you. And your mother's family must stand aside and do nothing. But it's always the same story. The more you do, the less thanks you get and the more you're expected to go on doing. Your uncle always pretended to be fond of you. But when it comes to parting with any money he's so stingy that rather than do it he makes up all these outrageous lies.'

'Well, you won't have to bother,' I said. 'You won't have to give me any more money. Or Uncle Bo or anybody else either. I can get all the money I want and so that's all right. Is everybody happy? Yes, everybody's happy.'

She stared at me. Her eyes had an inquisitive look and then a cold, disgusted look.

I said, 'If you want to know, I –'

'I don't want to know,' she said. 'You tell me that you hope to get an engagement in London. That's all I want to know. I intend to write to your uncle and tell him that I refuse to be made responsible for you. If he thinks you're not living in a fit and proper way he must do something to stop it himself; I can't. I've always done my duty, and more than my duty, but there does come a time when –'

'The brooch has fallen down,' I said. I picked it up and put it on the table.

'Oh, thank you,' she said.

And I saw her getting calm. I knew that she was saying to herself, 'I'm never going to think of this again.'

'I can't discuss it any more today,' she said. 'I'm too much upset about that letter. But I believe that everything that's necessary has been said. I'm going back to Yorkshire tomorrow, but I hope you'll write and tell me how you get on. I advise you to let your uncle know that I've shown you his letter. I hope you'll get this engagement you're trying for.'

'I hope so too,' I said

'I'll always be glad to do what I can for you. But if it's a question of money, please remember that I've already done far more than I can afford.'

'You needn't worry about that,' I said. 'I won't ask you for money.'

She didn't say anything for a bit and then she said, 'Have some tea before you go.'

'No, thanks,' I said.

She didn't kiss me when I said, 'Good-bye.'

She always hated Francine.

'What do you talk about?' she used to say.

'We don't talk about anything,' I'd say. 'We just talk.'

But she didn't believe me.

'That girl ought to be sent away,' she said to Father.

'Send Francine away?' Father said. 'What, send away a girl who can cook as well as she can. My dear Hester!'

The thing about Francine was that when I was with her I was happy. She was small and plump and blacker than most of the people out there, and she had a pretty face. What I liked was watching her eat mangoes. Her teeth would bite into the mango and her lips fasten on either side of it, and while she sucked you saw that she was perfectly happy. When she had finished she always smacked her lips twice, very loud – louder than you could believe possible. It was a ritual.

She never wore shoes and the soles of her feet were hard as leather. She could carry anything on her head – a bottleful of water, or a huge weight. Hester used to say, 'What are these people's heads made of? A white man couldn't carry a weight like that. Their heads must be like blocks of wood or something.'

She was always laughing, but when she sang it sounded sad. Even very gay, quick tunes sounded sad. She would sit for a long while singing to herself, and 'beating tambou lé-lé' – a thump with the base of the hand and then five short knocks with the fingers.

I don't know how old she was and she didn't know either. Sometimes they don't. But anyhow she was a bit older than I was and when I was unwell for the first time it was she who explained to me, so that it seemed quite all right and I thought it was all in the day's work like eating or drinking. But then she went off and told Hester, and Hester came and jawed away at me, her eyes wandering all over the place. I kept saying, 'No, rather not. . . . Yes, I see. . . . Oh yes, of course. . . .' But I began to feel awfully miserable, as if everything were shutting up around me and I couldn't breathe. I wanted to die.

After she had finished talking I went on to the verandah and lay in the hammock and swung. We were up at Morgan's Rest. Hester and I were there by ourselves, for Father had gone away for a week. I can remember every minute of that day.

The ropes of the hammock creaked and there was a wind and the outer shutters kept banging, like guns. It was shut-in there, between two hills, like the end of the world. It had not rained for some time and the grass on the crête was burnt brown in the sun.

When I had swung for a bit I felt very sick. So I stopped the hammock and lay there, looking at the sea. There were white lines on it, as if ships had just passed.

At half-past twelve we had breakfast and Hester started talking about Cambridge. She was always talking about Cambridge.

She said she was sure I should like England very much and that it would be a very good thing for me if I were to go to England. And then she talked about her uncle who was fifth wrangler and people used to call him 'Dirty Watts'.

'He was rather dirty,' she said, 'but it was simply absent-mindedness. And his wife, Aunt Fanny, was a beauty – a great beauty. One evening at the theatre when she entered her box everybody stood up. Spontaneously.'

'Fancy!' I said. 'My goodness!'

'Don't say my goodness,' Hester said. 'My badness, that's what you ought to say.'

'Yes, Beauty and the Beast, people used to call them,' she said. 'Beauty and the Beast. Oh, there were many stories about her. There was the young man who answered when she was annoyed at him staring at her:

> "A cat may look at a king,
>   So why not I at a prettier thing?"

She was very pleased at that and she often told the story, and the young man became a great favourite – a very great favourite. Let me see – what was his name? In any case he was at King's. Was it King's or Trinity? I can't remember. However, he was quite a wit in his way and she liked witty people; she forgave them anything. People took the trouble to be witty in those days. It's all very well to cry down those days but people were wittier then.'

'Yes,' I said. 'Like Judge Bryant the other night at the dance when some fool put his arm across the door of the supper-room and said, "Nobody pass who doesn't make a rhyme, nobody pass who doesn't make a rhyme." And Judge Bryant said, as quick as lightning:

> "Let us pass
> You damned old ass."

That was pretty quick, too, don't you think?'

Hester said, 'There's a certain difference, but of course you can't be expected to see that.' In that voice as if she were talking to herself.

We ate fishcakes and sweet potatoes and then we had stewed guavas; and bread-fruit instead of bread because she liked to feel that she was eating bread-fruit.

Sitting there eating you could see the curve of a hill like the curve of a green shoulder. And there were pink roses on the table in a curly blue vase with gold rings.

There was a chest in the corner where the drinks were kept and a sideboard ranged with glasses. And the bookshelf with Walter Scott and a lot of old Longmans' Magazines, so old that the pages were yellow.

After breakfast I went back into the verandah and she came there too and sat down in a long canvas chair. She began to stroke Scamp and to blink her eyes, like when she asked conundrums. (Who did Hall Caine? Dorothea Baird.) Scamp fawned on her.

'I hate dogs,' I said.

'Well, really!' she said.

'Well, I do,' I said.

'I don't know what'll become of you if you go on like that,' Hester said. 'Let me tell you that you'll have a very unhappy life if you go on like that. People won't like you. People in England will dislike you very much if you say things like that.'

'I don't care,' I said. But I began to repeat the multiplication-table because I was afraid I was going to cry.

Then I got up and told her I was going to the kitchen to speak to Francine.

The kitchen was about twenty yards away – a shingled, two-roomed house. One of the rooms was Francine's bedroom. There was a bed in it, and an earthenware pitcher and basin and a chair, and above the bed a lot of pictures of Jesus with the Sacred Heart aflame with love, the Virgin Mary in blue with her arms outstretched, and so on. 'St Joseph, priez pour nous.' 'Jesus, Mary, Joseph, grant me the grace of a happy death.'

When she wasn't working Francine would sit on the doorstep and I liked sitting there with her. Sometimes she told me stories, and at the start of the story she had to say 'Timm, timm,' and I had to answer 'Bois sèche.'

You looked across a path, sometimes muddy when it had been raining, or dry, with open, gaping cracks as if the earth were thirsty, at a clump of bamboos swinging in the sun or the rain. But the kitchen was horrible. There was no chimney and it was always full of charcoal-smoke.

Francine was there, washing up. Her eyes were red with the smoke and watering. Her face was quite wet. She wiped her eyes with the back of her hand and looked sideways at me. Then she said something in patois and went on washing up. But I knew that of course she disliked me too because I was white; and that I would never be able to explain to her that I hated being white. Being white and getting like Hester, and all the things you get – old and sad and everything. I kept thinking, 'No. ... No. ... No. ...' And I knew that day that I'd started to grow old and nothing could stop it.

I went on without looking at her again, past the rose-beds and the big mango tree and up the hill. The doves were going all the time. It was about two o'clock, just when the sun was hottest.

It had a barren look, that place, a hot, frowning, barren look because of the big grey boulders lying about – an eruption a long time ago, they said. But I don't mean that it wasn't a beautiful place. It was good land – or my father always said it was. He grew cocoa and nutmegs. And coffee on the slopes of the hill.

When the young nutmeg trees flowered for the first time he used to take me with him to see if the tree was male or female, because the buds were so small that you had to have sharp eyes to see the difference. 'You're young and you have sharp eyes,' he would say. 'Come along.'

'I'm getting old,' he would say. 'My eyes aren't as good as they used to be.' I always felt so miserable when he said that.

I got well away from the house. I sat down against a

62

rock in the shadow. The sky was terribly blue and very close to the earth.

I felt I was more alone than anybody had ever been in the world before and I kept thinking, 'No. . . . No. . . . No. . . .' just like that. Then a cloud came in front of my eyes and seemed to blot out half of what I ought to have been able to see. It was always like that when I was going to have a headache.

I thought, 'Well, all right. This time I'll die.' So I took my hat off and went and stood in the sun.

The sun at home can be terrible, like God. This thing here – I can't believe it's the same sun, I simply can't believe it.

I stood there until I felt the pain of the headache begin and then the sky came up close to me. It clanged, it was so hard. The pain was like knives. And then I was cold, and when I had been very sick I went home.

I got fever and I was ill for a long time. I would get better and then it would start again. It went on for several months. I got awfully thin and ugly and yellow as a guinea, my father said.

I asked Hester if I had talked a lot when I was bad and she said, 'Yes, you talked about cats and a great deal about Francine.' It was after that she started disliking Francine so much and saying she ought to be sent away. I had to laugh when I thought that even after all this time she still had to drag Francine in.

I wrote once to Hester but she only sent me a postcard in reply, and after that I didn't write again. And she didn't either.

7

When it was sad was when you woke up at night and thought about being alone and that everybody says the man's bound to get tired. (You make up letters that you never send or even write. 'My darling Walter ...')

Everybody says, 'Get on.' Of course, some people do get on. Yes, but how many? What about what's-her-name? She got on, didn't she? 'Chorus-Girl Marries Peer's Son.' Well, *what* about her? Get on or get out, they say. Get on or get out.

What I want, Mr Price, is an effective song for a voice-trial. *Softly Awakes my Heart as the Flowers Awaken* – that's a very effective one.

Everybody says the man's bound to get tired and you read it in all books. But I never read now, so they can't get at me like that, anyway. ('My darling Walter ...')

When it was sad was when you lay awake, and then it began to get light and the sparrows started – that was when it was sad, a lonely feeling, a hopeless feeling. When the sparrows started to chirp.

But in the daytime it was all right. And when you'd had a drink you knew it was the best way to live in the world, because anything might happen. I don't know how people live when they know exactly what's going to happen to them each day. It seems to me it's better to be dead than to live like that. Dressing to go and meet him and coming out of the restaurant and the lights in the streets and getting into a taxi and when he kissed you in the taxi going there.

A month seemed like a week and I thought, 'It's June already.'

Sometimes it was hot that summer. The day we went to

Savernake it was really hot. I had been sitting out on Primrose Hill. There were swarms of children there. Just behind my chair a big boy and a little one were playing with a rope. The little one was being tied up elaborately, so that he couldn't move his arms or legs. When the big one gave him a push he fell flat. He lay on the ground, still laughing for a second. Then his face changed and he started to cry. The big boy kicked him – not hard. He yelled louder. 'Nah then,' the big one said. He got ready to kick again. But then he saw I was watching. He grinned and undid the rope. The little boy stopped crying and got up. They both put out their tongues at me and ran off. The little one's legs were short and dimpled. When he ran he could hardly keep up. However, he didn't forget to turn round and put his tongue out again as far as he could.

There was no sun, but the air was used-up and dead, dirty-warm, as if thousands of other people had breathed it before you. A woman passed, throwing a ball for a dog called Caesar. Her voice was like Hester's:

'See-zah, See-zah ...'

After a bit I went home and had a cold bath.

When Mrs Dawes came in with Walter's letter I was lying down doing breathing exercises. Price always said that when you were lying down was the time to do them.

'I'll call for you with the car at six o'clock. We're going into the country. Will you bring things for two days and everything else you need – you know?'

As I was going out Mrs Dawes came up from the basement.

'Good-bye,' I said. 'I'll be back on Monday or Tuesday.'

She said, 'Good-bye, Miss Morgan.' She had white hair, a long, placid face and a soft voice – not a cockney voice. She always made her expression blank when she spoke to me.

'I hope you'll enjoy yourself, I'm sure,' she said, and stood at the door watching me get into the car.

I was wondering if I looked all right, because I hadn't had time to dry my hair properly. I was so nervous about how I looked that three-quarters of me was in a prison, wandering round and round in a circle. If he had said that I looked all right or that I was pretty, it would have set me free. But he just looked me up and down and smiled.

'Vincent's coming down by train tomorrow and bringing a girl. I thought it might be fun.'

'Oh, is he?' I said. 'How nice. Is she the girl I met – Eileen?'

'No, not Eileen. Another girl.'

I got happier when it grew darker. A moth flew into my face and I hit at it and killed it.

There were stags' heads stuck up all over the dining-room of the hotel. The one over our table was as big as a cow's. Its enormous glass eyes stared past us. In the bedroom there were prints – 'The Sailor's Farewell', 'The Sailor's Return', 'Reading the Will' and 'Conjugal Affection'. They had a calm, sleepy look, as if they were drawings of stuffed figures – the women very tall and plump and smiling and tidy and the men with long legs and bushy whiskers; but the placid shapes of the trees made you feel that that time must have been a good time.

I woke up very early and couldn't think for a bit where I was. A cool smell, that wasn't the dead smell of London, came in through the window. Then I remembered that I hadn't got to get up and go away and that the next night I'd be there still and he'd be there. I was very happy, happier than I had ever been in my life. I was so happy that I cried, like a fool.

That day it was hot again. After lunch we went to Savernake Forest. The leaves of the beech trees were bright as glass in the sun. In the clearings there were quantities of little flowers in the grass, red, yellow, blue and white, so many that it looked all colours.

Walter said, 'Have you got flowers like these in your island? These little bright things are rather sweet, don't you think?'

I said, 'Not quite like these.' But when I began to talk about the flowers out there I got that feeling of a dream, of two things that I couldn't fit together, and it was as if I were making up the names. Stephanotis, hibiscus, yellow-bell, jasmine, frangipanni, corolita.

I said, 'Flamboyant trees are lovely when they're flowering.'

There was a lark rising jerkily, as if it went by clockwork, as if someone were winding it up and stopping every now and again.

Walter said, as if he were talking to himself, 'No imagination? That's all rot. I've got a lot of imagination. I've wanted to bring you to Savernake and see you underneath these trees ever since I've known you.'

'I like it here,' I said. 'I didn't know England could be so beautiful.'

But something had happened to it. It was as if the wildness had gone out of it.

We got to where the beech trees grew close together and their branches met, high up. You had the feeling that outside it was a hot, blue day.

We went and sat on a tree that had fallen down, with its roots still partly in the earth. There wasn't enough wind for you to hear the trees. For a long time we didn't say anything. I was thinking how happy I was, and then I didn't think anything – not even how happy I was.

He said, 'You're lovely from this angle.'

'Not from every angle?' I said.

'Certainly not, conceited child. But from this angle you're perfectly satisfactory, and I want very much to make love to you. There are a lot of holes where the deer shelter in winter and where nobody could see us.'

I said, 'Oh no, not here. Just imagine if anybody saw us.' I heard myself giggling.

He said, 'But nobody would. And what if they did? They'd think "these two people are perfectly happy", and be jealous of us and leave us alone.'

I said, 'Well, they might be like that about it, or they mightn't.' I was thinking, 'When we go back to the hotel ...'

'Shy, Anna,' he said.

'Let's go back to the hotel, anyway,' I said. (You shut the door and you pull the curtains over the windows and then it's as long as a thousand years and yet so soon ended. Laurie saying, 'Some women don't start liking it till they are getting old; that's a bit of bad luck if you like. I'd rather wear myself out while I'm young.')

'My God, yes,' he said. 'That reminds me. Vincent must be there by now. I expect he's waiting for us.'

I had forgotten about Vincent.

'Come on,' Walter said.

We got up. I felt cold, like when you've been asleep and have just woken up.

'You'll like the girl he's bringing with him,' he said. 'Germaine Sullivan, her name is. I'm sure you'll like her. She's an awfully good sort.'

'Is she?' Then I couldn't help saying, 'Vincent isn't.'

'You don't mean to say you don't like Vincent?' he said. 'You're the only girl I've heard of who doesn't.'

'Of course I like him. He's certainly very good-looking,' I said. 'Is this girl on the stage too?'

'No,' Walter said. 'Vincent met her in Paris. She says she's half-French. God knows what she is; she might be anything. But she really is rather amusing.'

We found the car and went back to the hotel. It was nearly six o'clock. I kept thinking, 'It's unlucky to know you're happy; it's unlucky to say you're happy. Touch wood. Cross my fingers. Spit.'

Vincent said, 'Well, how's the child? How's my infantile Anna?'

He was very good-looking. He had blue eyes with curled-up eyelashes like a girl's, and black hair and a brown face and broad shoulders and slim hips – the whole bag of tricks, in fact. He was a bit like Walter, only younger. And better-looking, I suppose. At least, his face was better-looking. He looked about twenty-five but he was thirty-one really, Walter told me.

'We were wondering what had become of you,' the girl said. 'We've been here nearly two hours. We thought you'd left us in the lurch. I was thinking of finding out if there's a train back.'

She was pretty, but she looked as if they had been quarrelling.

'She's in a very bad temper,' Vincent said. 'I don't know what's upset her.'

I went upstairs to change my dress. I put on a dress with a flower-pattern that I had bought at Maud Moore's. The shadows of the leaves on the wall were moving quickly, like the patterns the sun makes on water.

'Look at this thing over the table,' Germaine said. 'This stag or whatever it is. It's exactly like your sister, Vincent, horns and all. D'you remember that time I bumped into her by mistake just outside your flat? Wasn't it funny?'

Vincent didn't answer.

'You think you're perfect, don't you?' Germaine said. 'Well, you're not perfect. Whenever you drink champagne you belch. I was ashamed of you the other night. You go like this.'

She imitated him. The waiter, who was on the other

side of the room, heard; and he looked across at us with a shocked expression, pursing his mouth up.

'Did you see that face?' Germaine said. 'Well, that's the way you look sometimes, Vincent. Scorn and loathing of the female – a very common expression in this country. Imitation gold-fish, very difficult.'

'I wouldn't be an Englishwoman,' she said, 'for any money you could give me or anything else.'

'Opportunity's a fine thing,' Vincent said, smiling a little.

She shut up a bit after that, but when we were having more drinks in the lounge she started off again about England. 'It's a very nice place,' she said, 'so long as you don't suffer from claustrophobia.'

'Once,' she said, 'a very clever man said to me ...'

'A Frenchman, of course,' Vincent said. 'Come on, let's hear what the very clever Frenchman said.'

'Shut up,' Germaine said. 'What he said was quite true. He said that there were pretty girls in England, but very few pretty women. "In fact, hardly any," he said, "I don't believe there are any. Why? What happens to them? A few pretty girls and then finish, a blank, a desert. What happens to them?" '

'And it's true too,' she said. 'The women here are awful. That beaten, cringing look – or else as cruel and dried-up as they're made! Méchantes, that's what they are. And everybody knows why they're like that. They're like that because most Englishmen don't care a damn about women. They can't make women happy because they don't really like them. I suppose it's the climate or something. Well, thank God, it doesn't matter much to me one way or the other.'

Vincent said, 'Can't they, Germaine? Can't they make women happy?' His face was smooth and smiling.

She got up and looked at herself in the glass. 'I'm going upstairs for a minute,' she said.

'Going to curl your hair?' Vincent said. 'I'm sure you'll find the curl-papers there all right.'

She went out without answering.

Walter said, 'The demoiselle seems annoyed about something. What's the matter with her?'

'Oh, she thinks I ought to have told her before,' Vincent said, 'and she's cut up rough about one thing and another. She started the argument on the way down here. She was all right before that. It'll end in a flood of tears. As usual.'

I hated the way they were looking at each other. I got up.

'Are you also going to curl your hair?' Vincent said.

'No,' I said, 'I'm going to the lavatory.'

'Good for you,' he said.

It seemed a long time since the morning, I was thinking. Last night I was so happy that I cried, like a fool. Last night I was happy.

I looked out of the bedroom window and there was a thin mist coming up from the ground. It was very still.

Before I came to England I used to try to imagine a night that was quite still. I used to try to imagine it with the crac-cracs going. The verandah long and ghostly – the hammock and three chairs and a table with the telescope on it – and the crac-cracs going all the time. The moon and the darkness and the sound of the trees, and not far away the forest where nobody had ever been – virgin forest. We used to sit on the verandah with the night coming in, huge. And the way it smelt of all flowers. ('This place gives me the creeps at night,' Hester would say.)

I was standing in front of the long glass in the bedroom when Walter came in.

He said, 'D'you mind if we go back to London tonight?'

I said, 'I thought the idea was that we were going to

stay here tonight and go on to Oxford tomorrow morning.'

'That was the idea,' Walter said. 'But they've had an awful fight and now Germaine says she doesn't want to stay. She says this place gives her the pip.'

'And she's been very rude about Oxford,' he said, starting to laugh. 'I think we'd better take them up tonight. You don't mind, do you?'

'All right,' I said.

'You're sure you don't mind?'

'No,' I said. I began to put my things into the suitcase.

'Oh, leave that,' Walter said. 'The maid will do it. Come downstairs and talk to Germaine. You like her, don't you?'

I said, 'Yes, I like her all right, if she'd only stop going for Vincent all the time.'

'She's very much annoyed with him,' Walter said.

'Yes, I can see she's annoyed. Why? What's the matter with her?'

He put his hands in his pockets and stood rocking backwards and forwards. He said, 'I don't know. Bad temper, I suppose. Vincent's going away next week for some time and she seems to have got into a bad temper over it. The fact is, she wants him to leave her more money than he can afford.'

'Oh, is he going away?' I said. I was still looking in the glass.

He said, 'Yes, I'm going to New York next week and I'm taking him with me.'

I didn't say anything. I put my face nearer the glass. Like when you're a kid and you put your face very near to the glass and make faces at yourself.

'I won't be gone long,' he said. 'I'll be back in a couple of months at the outside.'

'Oh, I see,' I said.

The maid knocked at the door and came in.

We went downstairs and had another drink. 'Drink's pretty nice,' I thought.

Vincent began to talk about books. He said, 'I read a good book the other day – a damned fine book. When I read it I thought, "The man who wrote this should be knighted." *The Rosary*, it was called.'

'A woman wrote that book, you fool,' Walter said.

'Oh?' Vincent said. 'Good Lord! Well, even if a woman wrote it she should be knighted, that's all I can say. That's what I call a fine book.'

'He ought to be put in a glass case, oughtn't he?' Germaine said. 'The perfect specimen.'

Walter said, 'Well, I'd better go and see about the car.'

Germaine was staring at me. 'She looks awfully young, this kid,' she said. 'She looks about sixteen.'

'Yes,' Vincent said. 'Dear old Walter, whom we all know and love, has been doing a bit of baby-snatching, I'm afraid.'

'How old are you?' Germaine said, and I told her, 'Nineteen.'

'She's going to be a great girl one of these days,' Vincent said, putting on his kind expression. 'We're trying to make a start in the autumn, aren't we, Anna? The new show at Daly's. You ought to be able to warble like what's-her-name after all those singing lessons.'

'She's on the stage, is she?' Germaine said.

'Yes, she is or was. You were in a show when you first met Walter, weren't you?' Vincent said.

'Yes,' I said.

They looked at me as if they were expecting me to say something else.

'It was at Southsea,' I said.

'Oh, it was at Southsea, was it?' Vincent said.

They began to laugh. They were still laughing when Walter came in.

'She's been giving you away,' Vincent said. 'She's been telling us how it all started. You dirty dog, Walter. What in God's name were you doing on the pier at Southsea?'

Walter blinked. Then he said, 'You shouldn't let Vincent pump you. He's as inquisitive as an old woman. You wouldn't think it to look at him, but he is.'

He started to laugh too.

'Shut up laughing,' I said.

I thought, 'Shut up laughing,' looking at Walter's hand hanging over the edge of the mantelpiece.

I said, 'Oh, stop laughing at me. I'm sick of it.'

'What's the joke?' I said.

They went on laughing.

I was smoking, and I put the end of my cigarette down on Walter's hand. I jammed it down hard and held it there, and he snatched his hand away and said 'Christ!' But they had stopped laughing.

'Bravo, kid,' Germaine said, 'Bravo.'

'Calm down,' Walter said. 'What's all the excitement about?' He didn't look at me.

'Oh God,' Vincent said. 'Let's get off, shall we?'

We got into the car. Germaine sat next Walter in the front and Vincent and I were at the back.

Vincent started off again about books.

I said, 'I haven't read any of these books you're talking about. I hardly ever read.'

'Well, what do you do with yourself all day?' he said.

'I don't know,' I said.

I said, 'You're going to New York, aren't you?'

He cleared his throat and said, 'Yes, we're going next week.'

I didn't say anything, and he squeezed my hand and said, 'Don't worry. You'll be all right.'

I pulled my hand away. I thought, 'No, I don't like you.'

74

We stopped at Germaine's flat.

I said, 'Good night, Germaine. Good night, Vincent; thank you very much.' What did I say that for? I thought. I'm always being stupid with this man. I bet he'll make me feel I've said something stupid.

And sure enough he raised his eyebrows, 'Thank me very much? My dear child, why thank me very much?'

'Well,' Walter said. 'where shall we go now? Let's go and have some supper somewhere.'

I said, 'No, let's go back to your house.'

He said, 'Very well. All right.'

We went into a little room on the ground floor and had whiskies-and-sodas and sandwiches. It was stiffly furnished – I didn't like it much. There was a damned bust of Voltaire, stuck up on a shelf, sneering away. There are all sorts of sneers, of course, the high and the low.

I said, 'Germaine's awfully pretty.'

'She's old,' he said.

'I bet she isn't; I bet she isn't any older than Vincent.'

'Well, that is old for a woman. Besides, she'll be blowsy in another year; she's that type.'

'Anyway, she was funny about English people,' I said. 'I liked what she said, rather.'

'I was disappointed in Germaine,' he said. 'I didn't think she could have been such a damned bore. She was simply kicking up a row because Vincent couldn't give her all the money she asked for, and as a matter of fact he's given her far more than he can afford – far more than anybody else would have given her. She thought she had her claws well into him. It's a very good thing he's going away.'

'Oh, has he given her far more than he can afford?' I said.

He said, 'By the way, why did you tell Vincent about Southsea? You shouldn't give yourself away like that.'

'But I didn't,' I said.

'But, my dear, you must have. Otherwise, how could he have known?'

'Well, I didn't think it mattered. He asked me.'

He said, 'My God, do you consider yourself bound to answer every question anybody asks you? That's a tall order.'

'I don't like this room much,' I said. 'I rather hate it. Let's go upstairs.'

He imitated me. 'Let's go upstairs, let's go upstairs. You really shock me sometimes, Miss Morgan.'

I wanted to pretend it was like the night before, but it wasn't any use. Being afraid is cold like ice, and it's like when you can't breathe. 'Afraid of what?' I thought.

Just before I got up to go I said, 'You don't know how miserable I am about your hand.'

'Oh, that!' he said. 'It doesn't matter.'

There was the clock ticking all the time on a table by the bed.

I said, 'Listen. Don't forget me, don't forget me ever.'

He said, 'No, I won't ever, I tell you,' as if he were afraid I was getting hysterical. I got up and dressed.

My bag was on the table. He took it up and put some money into it. I watched him.

He said, 'I don't know whether we can meet again before I leave London, because I'm going to be most awfully busy. Anyhow, I'll write to you tomorrow. About money. I want you to go away for a change somewhere. Where would you like to go?'

'I don't know,' I said. 'I'll go somewhere.'

He turned round and said, 'Hello, is anything wrong? Don't you feel well?'

'Extraordinary thing,' I was thinking. I felt sick and my forehead was wet.

I said, 'I'm all right. Good-bye for now. Don't bother to come with me.'

'Of course I'm coming with you,' he said.

We went downstairs. When he opened the door there was a taxi passing and he stopped it.

Then he said, 'Come back in here for one minute. Are you sure you're all right?'

I said, 'Yes, quite.'

There was that damned bust smiling away.

'Well, good-bye,' he said. He coughed. 'Take care of yourself.'

'Bless you,' he said and coughed again.

'Oh, yes. Oh, rather,' I said.

I wasn't sleepy. I looked out of the window of the taxi. Men were watering the streets and there was a fresh smell, like an animal just bathed.

When I got home I lay down without undressing. Then it got light and I thought that when Mrs Dawes came in with my breakfast she would think I had gone mad. So I got up and undressed.

'This is no way for a young girl to live,' Mrs Dawes said.

That was because for a week after Walter left I hadn't gone out; I didn't want to. What I liked was lying in bed till very late, because I felt tired all the time, and having something to eat in bed and then in the afternoon staying a long time in the bath. I would put my head under the water and listen to the noise of the tap running. I would pretend it was a waterfall, like the one that falls into the pool where we bathed at Morgan's Rest.

I was always dreaming about that pool, too. It was clear just beyond where the waterfall fell, but the shallow parts were very muddy. Those big white flowers that open at night grew round it. Pop-flowers, we call them. They are shaped like lilies and they smell heavy-sweet, very strong. You can smell them a long way off. Hester couldn't bear the scent, it made her faint. There were crabs under the rocks by the river. I used to splash when I bathed because of them. They have small eyes at the end of long feelers, and when you throw stones at them their shells smash and soft, white stuff bubbles out. I was always dreaming about this pool and seeing the green-brown water in my dream.

'No, this is no way for a young girl to live,' Mrs Dawes said.

People say 'young' as though being young were a crime, and yet they are always so scared of getting old. I thought, 'I wish I were old and the whole damned thing were finished; then I shouldn't get this depressed feeling for nothing at all.'

I didn't know what to answer. She was always like that – placid and speaking softly, but a bit as if she were watching me sideways. When I told her that I wanted to get away for a change, she said she had a cousin in Minehead who let rooms, so I went there.

But after three weeks I went back to London because I had a letter from Walter saying that he might be in England again sooner than he had expected. And one day at the beginning of October, when I came in after walking about Primrose Hill in the rain (nothing but the damp trees and the soggy grass and the sad, slow-moving clouds – it's funny how it makes you feel that there's not anything else anywhere, that it's all made up that there is anything else), Mrs Dawes said, 'There's a letter for you. I took it up to your room. I thought you was in.'

I got upstairs. It was lying on the table, and right across the room I thought, 'Who on earth's that from?' because of the handwriting.

8

... I was walking along the passage to the long upper verandah which ran the length of the house in town – there were four upstairs bedrooms two on either side of the passage – the boards were not painted and the knots in the wood were like faces – Uncle Bo was in the verandah lying on the sofa his mouth was a bit open – I thought he's asleep and I started to walk on tiptoe – the blinds were down all except one so that you could see the broad leaves of the sandbox tree – I got up to the table where the magazine was and Uncle Bo moved and sighed and long yellow tusks like fangs came out of his mouth and protruded down to his chin – you don't scream when you are frightened because you can't and you don't move either because you can't – after a long time he sighed and opened his eyes and clicked his teeth back into place and said what on earth do you want child – it was the magazine I said – he turned over and went to sleep again – I went out very softly – I had never seen false teeth before not to notice them – I shut the door and went away very softly down the passage ...

I thought, 'But what's the matter with me? That was years and years ago, ages and ages ago. Twelve years ago or something like that. What's this letter got to do with false teeth?'

I read it again:

My dear Anna,
This is a very difficult letter to write because I am afraid I am going to upset you and I hate upsetting people. We've been back for nearly a week but Walter hasn't been at all well and I have persuaded him to let me write to you and explain matters. I'm quite sure you are a nice girl and that you will be understanding about this. Walter is still very fond of you but he

doesn't love you like that any more, and after all you must always have known that the thing could not go on for ever and you must remember too that he is nearly twenty years older than you are. I'm sure that you are a nice girl and that you will think it over calmly and see that there is nothing to be tragic or unhappy or anything like that about. You are young and youth as everybody says is the great thing, the greatest gift of all. The greatest gift, everybody says. And so it is. You've got everything in front of you, lots of happiness. Think of that. Love is not everything – especially that sort of love – and the more people, especially girls, put it right out of their heads and do without it the better. That's my opinion. Life is chock-full of other things, my dear girl, friends and just good times and being jolly together and so on and games and books. Do you remember when we talked about books? I was sorry when you told me that you never read because, believe me, a good book like that book I was talking about can make a lot of difference to your point of view. It makes you see what is real and what is just imaginary. My dear Infant, I am writing this in the country, and I can assure you that when you get into a garden and smell the flowers and all that all this rather beastly sort of love simply doesn't matter. However, you will think I'm preaching at you, so I will shut up. These muddles do happen. They have happened to me, as a matter of fact, worse luck. I can't think why. I can't think why one can't be more sensible. However, I have learnt one thing, that it never helps to let things drag on. Walter has asked me to enclose this cheque for £20 for your immediate expenses because he thinks you may be running short of cash. He will always be your friend and he wants to arrange that you should be provided for and not have to worry about money (for a time at any rate). Write and let him know that you understand. If you really care for him at all you will do this, for believe me he is unhappy about you and he has a lot of other worries as well. Or write me – that would be better still because don't you think it would be just as well for both your sakes if you don't see Walter just now? Then there's that job in the new show. I want to take you along as soon as possible to see my friend. I think I can promise you that something will come of it. I believe that if you will work hard there is no reason why you should not get on. I've always said that and I stick to it.

Yours ever,
Vincent Jeffries.

P.S. Have you kept any of the letters Walter wrote to you? If so you ought to send them back.

I thought, 'What the hell's the matter with me? I must be crazy. This letter has nothing to do with false teeth.'

But I went on thinking about false teeth, and then about piano-keys and about that time the blind man from Martinique came to tune the piano and then he played and we listened to him sitting in the dark with the jalousies shut because it was pouring with rain and my father said, 'You are a real musician.' He had a red moustache, my father. And Hester was always saying, 'Poor Gerald, poor Gerald.' But if you'd seen him walking up Market Street, swinging his arms and with his brown shoes flashing in the sun, you wouldn't have been sorry for him. That time when he said, 'The Welsh word for grief is hiraeth.' Hiraeth. And that time when I was crying about nothing and I thought he'd be wild, but he hugged me up and he didn't say anything. I had on a coral brooch and it got crushed. He hugged me up and then he said, 'I believe you're going to be like me, you poor little devil.' And that time when Mr Crowe said, 'You don't mean to say you're backing up that damned French monkey?' meaning the Governor, 'I've met some Englishmen,' he said, 'who were monkeys too.'

When I looked at the clock it was a quarter past five. I had been sitting there like that for two hours. I thought, 'Go on, get up,' and after a while I went to a post-office and wrote out a telegram to Walter: 'I would like to see you tonight if possible please Anna.'

Then I went back home. My hands were very cold and I kept rubbing them together.

I thought, 'He won't answer, and I don't care, because I don't want to have to move again.' But at half past seven Mrs Dawes brought up a telegram from him: 'Meet me tonight Central Hotel Marylebone Road 9.30 Walter.'

9

I dressed very carefully. I didn't think of anything while I dressed. I put on my black velvet dress and made up a bit with rather more rouge than usual and when I looked in the glass I thought, 'He won't be able to, he won't be able to.' There was a lump in my throat. I kept swallowing it, but it came back again.

It was pouring with rain. Mrs Dawes was in the hall.

'You'll get wet,' she said. 'I'll send Willie as far as the Tube station to get a taxi for you.'

'Thank you,' I said.

There was a chair in the hall and I sat there and waited.

Willie was gone a long time and Mrs Dawes began to click her tongue and mutter, 'The poor boy – out in the pouring rain. Some people give a lot of trouble.'

I sat there. I had a shrunken feeling just like having fever. I thought, 'When you have fever your feet burn like fire but your hands are clammy.'

Then the taxi came; and the houses on either side of the street were small and dark and then they were big and dark but all exactly alike. And I saw that all my life I had known that this was going to happen, and that I'd been afraid for a long time, I'd been afraid for a long time. There's fear, of course, with everybody. But now it had grown, it had grown gigantic; it filled me and it filled the whole world.

I was thinking, 'I ought to have given Willie a bob. I know Mrs Dawes was annoyed because I didn't give him a bob. It was just that I didn't think of it. Tomorrow some time I must get hold of him and give him a bob.'

Then the taxi got into Marylebone Road and I remembered that once I had been to a flat in Marylebone Road and there were three flights of stairs and then a small room and it smelt musty. The room had smelt musty and through the glass of a window that wouldn't open you saw dark green trees.

The taxi stopped and I got down and paid the man and went into the hotel.

He was waiting for me.

I smiled and said, 'Hullo.'

He had been looking very solemn but when I smiled like that he seemed relieved.

We went and sat in a corner.

I said, 'I'll have coffee.'

I imagined myself saying, very calmly, 'The thing is that you don't understand. You think I want more than I do. I only want to see you sometimes, but if I never see you again I'll die. I'm dying now really, and I'm too young to die.'

... The candles crying wax tears and the smell of stephanotis and I had to go to the funeral in a white dress and white gloves and a wreath round my head and the wreath in my hands made my gloves wet – they said so young to die ...

The people there were like upholstered ghosts.

I said, 'That letter I had from Vincent –'

'I knew he was writing,' he said, twisting his head a bit. 'You asked him to write?'

'Yes, I asked him to write.'

When he talked his eyes went away from mine and then he forced himself to look straight at me and he began to explain and I knew that he felt very strange with me and that he hated me, and it was funny sitting there and talking like that, knowing he hated me.

I said, 'All right. Listen, will you do something for me?'

'Of course,' he said. 'Anything. Anything you ask.'

I said, 'Well, will you get a taxi, please, and let's go back to your place, because I want to talk to you and I can't here.' I thought, 'I'll hang on to your knees and make you understand and then you won't be able to, you won't be able to.'

He said, 'Why do you ask me the one thing you know perfectly well I won't do?'

I didn't answer. I was thinking, 'You don't know anything about me. I don't care any more.' And I didn't care any more.

It was like letting go and falling back into water and seeing yourself grinning up through the water, your face like a mask, and seeing the bubbles coming up as if you were trying to speak from under the water. And how do you know what it's like to try to speak from under water when you're drowned? 'And I've met a lot of them who were monkeys too,' he said . . .

Walter was saying, 'I'm horribly worried about you. I want you to let Vincent come and see you and arrange things. I've talked it over with him and we've arranged things.'

I said, 'I don't want to see Vincent.'

'But why?' he said.

'I've talked it over with him,' he said. 'He knows how I feel about you.'

I said, 'I hate Vincent.'

He said, 'But, my dear, you don't imagine, do you, that Vincent's had anything to do with this?'

'He had,' I said, 'he had. D'you think I don't know he's been trying to put you against me ever since he saw me? D'you think I don't know?'

He said, 'It's a damned poor compliment to me if you think I'd let Vincent or anybody else interfere with me.'

'As a matter of fact,' he said, 'Vincent's hardly ever spoken about you. Except that he said once he thought you were very young and didn't quite know your way about and that it was a bit of a shame.'

I said, 'I know the sort of things he says; I can hear him saying them. D'you think I don't know?'

He said, 'I can't stand any more of this.'

'All right,' I said, 'let's go.'

I got up and we went out.

I got a taxi outside the hotel. I felt all right except that I was tired and I couldn't sit up straight. When he said, 'O God, look what I've done,' I wanted to laugh.

'I don't know what you mean,' I said. 'You haven't done anything.'

He said, 'You've got hold of absolutely the wrong end of the stick about Vincent. He's awfully fond of you and he wants to help you.'

I looked through the taxi-window and said, 'Hell to your beloved Vincent. Tell him to keep his bloody help. I don't want it.'

He looked shocked, like that waiter, when he said, 'Corked, sir?'

He said, 'I shouldn't wonder if I got ill with all this worry.'

When Mrs Dawes came in with breakfast I was lying on the bed with all my clothes on. I hadn't even taken off my shoes. She didn't say anything, she didn't look surprised, and when she looked at me I knew she was thinking, 'There you are. I always knew this would happen.' I imagined I saw her smile as she turned away.

I said, 'I'm leaving today. I'm sorry. I've had bad news. Will you let me have my bill?'

'Yes, Miss Morgan,' she said, her face long and placid. 'Yes, Miss Morgan.'

'Will you give Willie this five bob?' I said. 'Because he was always getting taxis for me.'

'Yes, Miss Morgan,' she said, 'I will, certainly.'

'I'll come back for my luggage in an hour or two,' I said.

I had fifteen pounds left after I had paid Mrs Dawes. I wrote a letter to Walter and asked her to post it:

Dear Walter,

Don't write here because I'm leaving. I'll let you know my new address.

Yours,
Anna.

I got out into the street. A man passed. I thought he looked at me funnily and I wanted to run, but I stopped myself.

I walked straight ahead. I thought, 'Anywhere will do, so long as it's somewhere that nobody knows.'

Part Two

I

There were two slices of dark meat on one plate, two potatoes and some cabbage. On the other plate a slice of bread and a lemon-cheese tart.

'I've brought you up the bottle of vermouth and the siphon you asked for,' the landlady said. This one had bulging eyes, dark blobs in a long, pink face, like a prawn. 'Well, you do write a lot of letters, don't you?' 'Yes,' I said. I put my hand over the sheet of paper I was writing on. 'Work quite 'ard, you do.' I didn't answer and she stood there for a bit, looking at me. 'Do you feel better to-day?' she said. 'You've 'ad influenza, p'raps?' 'Yes,' I said.

She went out. She was exactly like our landlady at Eastbourne. Was it Eastbourne? And the shapes of the slices of meat were the same, and the way the cabbage was heaped was the same, and all the houses outside in the street were the same – all alike, all hideously stuck together – and the streets going north, east, south, west, all exactly the same.

I wasn't hungry but I poured out a glass of vermouth and drank it without soda and went on writing. There were sheets of paper spread all over the bed.

After a while I crossed out everything and began again, writing very quickly, like you do when you write: 'You can't possibly do this you simply don't know what you're doing if I were a dog you wouldn't do this I love you I love you I love you but you're just a god-damned rotter everybody is everybody is everybody is – My dear Walter I've read books about this and I know quite well what you're thinking but you're quite wrong because don't you remember you used to joke because every time you put your hand on my heart it used to jump well you can't pretend that can you you can pretend everything else but not that it's the only thing you can't pretend I do want to ask you one thing I'd like to see you just once more listen it needn't be for very long it need only be for an hour well not an hour then half an hour ...' And going on like that, and the sheets of paper all over the bed.

The water-jug was broken. I thought, 'I bet she'll say I did that and want me to pay for it.'

The room was at the back of the house, so there were no street noises to listen to, but you could sometimes hear cats fighting or making love, and in the morning voices in the passages outside: 'She says she's ill. . . . What's the matter with 'er? ... She says she's 'ad flu. ... She says ...'

I kept the curtains drawn all the time. The window was like a trap. If you wanted to open or shut it you had to call in somebody to help you. The mantelshelf was crowded with china ornaments – several dogs of various breeds, a pig, a swan, a geisha with a kimono and sash in colours and a little naked woman lying on her stomach with a feather in her hair.

After a while I started to sing:

> 'Blow rings, rings
>   Delicate rings in the air;
> And drift, drift
>   – something – away from despair.'

That was a turn I had seen in a music-hall in Glasgow, where I had got in for a matinée on my card. The singer was a plump girl with very curly pale-gold hair but underneath it she had a long, stupid face. She went down very well.

> 'And drift, drift
>   Legions away from despair.'

It can't be 'legions'. 'Oceans', perhaps. 'Oceans away from despair.' But it's the sea, I thought. The Caribbean Sea. 'The Caribs indigenous to this island were a warlike tribe and their resistance to white domination, though spasmodic, was fierce. As lately as the beginning of the nineteenth century they raided one of the neighbouring islands, under British rule, overpowered the garrison and kidnapped the governor, his wife and three children. They are now practically exterminated. The few hundreds that are left do not intermarry with the Negroes. Their reservation, at the northern end of the island, is known as the Carib Quarter.' They had, or used to have, a king. Mopo, his name was. Here's to Mopo, King of the Caribs! But, they are now practically exterminated. 'Oceans away from despair. . . .'

I ate the lemon-cheese tart and began the song all over again. Somebody knocked at the door. I called out, 'Come in.'

It was the woman who had the room on the floor above. She was short and fat. She was wearing a white silk blouse and a dark skirt with stains on it and black stockings and patent-leather shoes and a dirty chemise which showed above her blouse. She had a long face and a long body and short legs, like they say the female should have. (And if she has hell to her because she's a female, and if she hasn't hell to her too, because she's probably not.) She had deep rings under her eyes and her hair looked dusty. She was about forty, but she moved about in a very spry way. She looked just like most other people, which is a big advantage. An ant, just like all the other ants; not the sort of ant that has too long a head or a deformed body or anything like that. She was like all women whom you look at and don't notice except that she had such short legs and that her hair was so dusty.

'Hullo,' she said. 'You don't mind me popping in, do you? Mrs Flower told me there was an ill young lady in this room. Do you feel bad?' she said, looking inquisitive. 'No, I'm all right. I'm better. I've had influenza,' I said. 'Let me put your tray outside. They'll leave it here till midnight. Sloppy, that's what they are. I'm a trained nurse and it gets on my nerves – all this sloppiness.'

She took the tray out and came back.

I said, 'Thank you very much. I'm all right really. I'm just going to get up.'

Then I said, 'No, don't go. Please stay.' Because after all she was a human being.

I got up and dressed, and she sat near the fire with her skirt pulled up and her short, plump, well-shaped legs exposed to the flames, and watched. Her eyes were cleverer than the rest of her. When she half-shut them you saw that she knew she had her own cunning, which would always save her, which was sufficient to her. Feelers grow when feelers are needed and claws when claws are needed and cunning when cunning is needed. . . .

I took all the sheets of paper off the bed and burnt them.

'You know, sometimes you can't get a letter written,' I said. 'I hate letters,' the woman said. 'I hate writing them and I hate getting them. If I don't see people I can't be bothered. My God, that's a lovely fur coat you have there, isn't it? . . . It's an awful day. If you've been ill and are going for a walk, really this isn't the day for it. Come along with me to the cinema in the Camden Town High Street, it's only a couple of minutes' walk. I know one of the girls in the crowd in the film that's on there. I want to see what she looks like.' She was staring at my coat all the time.

'My name's Matthews,' she said. 'Ethel Matthews.'

Just as we went into the cinema the lights went out and the screen flashed, 'Three-Fingered Kate, Episode 5. Lady Chichester's Necklace.'

The piano began to play, sickly-sweet. Never again,

never, not ever, never. Through caverns measureless to man down to a sunless sea . . .

The cinema smelt of poor people, and on the screen ladies and gentlemen in evening dress walked about with strained smiles.

'There!' Ethel said, nudging. 'D'you see that girl – the one with the band round her hair? That's the one I know; that's my friend. Do you see? My God, isn't she terrible? My God, what a scream!' 'Oh, shut up,' somebody said. 'Shut up yourself,' Ethel said.

I opened my eyes. On the screen a pretty girl was pointing a revolver at a group of guests. They backed away with their arms held high above their heads and expressions of terror on their faces. The pretty girl's lips moved. The fat hostess unclasped a necklace of huge pearls and fell, fainting, into the arms of a footman. The pretty girl, holding the revolver so that the audience could see that two of her fingers were missing, walked backwards towards the door. Her lips moved again. you could see what she was saying. 'Keep 'em up. . . .' When the police appeared everybody clapped. When Three-Fingered Kate was caught everybody clapped louder still.

'Damned fools,' I said. 'Aren't they damned fools? Don't you hate them? They always clap in the wrong places and laugh in the wrong places.'

'Three-Fingered Kate, Episode 6,' the screen said. 'Five Years Hard. Next Monday.' Then there was a long Italian film about the Empress Theodora, called 'The Dancer-Empress'. When it was finished I said, 'Let's go out. I don't want to stay any longer, do you?'

It was six o'clock, and when we got into Camden Town High Street it was quite dark. 'Not that there's much difference between the day and the night here, anyway,' I thought. The rain had stopped. The pavement looked as if it was covered with black grease.

Ethel said, 'Did you see that girl – the one who was

doing Three-Fingered Kate? Did you notice her hair? I mean, did you notice the curls she had on at the back?'

I was thinking, 'I'm nineteen and I've got to go on living and living and living.'

'Well,' she said, 'that girl who did Three-Fingered Kate was a foreigner. My friend who was working in the crowd told me about it. Couldn't they have got an English girl to do it?' 'Was she?' I said. 'Yes. Couldn't they have got an English girl to do it? It was just because she had this soft, dirty way that foreign girls have. And she stuck red curls on her black hair and she didn't care a scrap. Her own hair was short and black, don't you see? and she simply went and stuck red curls on. An English girl wouldn't have done that. Everybody was laughing at her behind her back, my friend said.' 'I didn't notice,' I said. 'I thought she was very pretty.' 'The thing is that red photographs black, d'you see? All the same, everybody was laughing at her behind her back all the time. Well, an English girl wouldn't have done that. An English girl would have respected herself more than to let people laugh at her like that behind her back.'

She got out her latchkey and said, 'Come on up to my room for a bit.'

Her room was exactly like mine except that her wallpaper was green instead of brown. She put some coal on the fire and sat down and pulled up her skirt. Her feet too were short and fat.

She said, 'Look here, kid, what's the matter with you? Are you in trouble? Are you going to have a baby or something? Because if you are you might as well tell me about it and I might be able to help you. You never know. Well, are you?'

'No,' I said, 'I'm not going to have a baby. What an idea!'

'What's the matter with you then?' Ethel said. 'What do you want to look so miserable about?'

'I'm not miserable,' I said. 'I'm all right, only I'd like a drink.

Ethel said, 'If that's all you want...'

She went to the cupboard and got out a gin-bottle and two glasses and poured out two drinks. I didn't touch mine, because the smell of gin always made me sick and because my eyeballs felt so big inside my head, and turning round like wheels. Who said, 'Oh Lord, let me see?' I would rather say, 'Oh Lord, keep me blind.'

'I hate men,' Ethel said. 'Men are devils, aren't they? But of course I don't really care a damn about them. Why should I? I can earn my own living. I'm a masseuse – I'm a Swedish masseuse. And, mind you, when I say I'm a masseuse I don't mean like some of these dirty foreigners. Don't you hate foreigners?'

'Well,' I said, 'I don't think I do; but, you see, I don't know many.'

'What?' Ethel said, looking surprised and suspicious, 'you don't hate them?'

She drank a little more. 'Well, of course, I know some girls like them. I knew a girl who was crazy about an Italian and she used to rave about him. She said he made her feel important when he made love to her. I ask you! And you should have heard her – it was too damned funny. Is your boy a foreigner?'

'No,' I said. 'Oh no. No.'

'Well,' Ethel said, 'don't go on looking like that – as if, as they say, Gawd 'ates yer and yer eyes don't fit.'

'That's like Maudie,' I said. 'My pal on tour. She used to say, "I feel as if God hates me and my eyes don't fit." '

'Oh, I see,' Ethel said, 'you're on the stage, are you?'

'A long time ago,' I said.

She said, 'Well, anyway, that's a wonderful coat you have.'

She felt my coat. Her little hands, with short, thick

fingers, felt it; and he ... 'Now perhaps you won't shiver so much,' he said.

'I bet you if you took that coat to Attenborough's they'd give you twenty-five quid on it. Well, perhaps they wouldn't give you twenty-five, but I bet they'd give you twenty. And that means its worth ...'

She began to giggle. 'People are such damned fools,' she said. 'I can't think why you stay in a room in Camden Town when you've got a coat like that.'

I drank the gin and almost as soon as I'd drunk it everything began to seem rather comical.

'Well, what are *you* here for then,' I said, 'if you think it's as awful as all that?'

'Oh, I don't need to be here,' she said haughtily. 'I've got a flat. I've got a flat in Bird Street. You know – just off Oxford Street, at the back of Selfridge's. I'm simply here while it's being done up.'

'Well, I don't need to be here either,' I said. 'I can get as much money as I like any time I like.' I stretched, and watched my swollen shadow on the wall stretching too.

She said, 'Well, I should say so – a lovely girl like you. And well under twenty, I should say. I've got a spare bedroom in my flat. Why don't you come along and live with me for a bit? I'm looking for somebody to share with me. As a matter of fact I'd almost fixed it up with a pal of mine. She'll put in twenty-five pounds and do the manicure and we'll start a little business.'

'Oh yes?' I said.

'Well, just between ourselves, I shan't mind if I don't fix it up with her. She's a bit of a Nosey Parker. Why don't you think it over? I've got a lovely spare room.'

'But I haven't got twenty-five pounds,' I said.

She said, 'You could get twenty pounds on that coat any day.'

'I don't want to sell my coat,' I said. 'And I don't know how to manicure.'

'Oh well, that's all right. I don't want to try to persuade you. Only come along and have a look at the room. I'm leaving tomorrow. I'll pop in and give you the address before I go.'

I said, 'I'm feeling a bit sleepy. I think I'll go along to my room. Good night.'

'Good night,' Ethel said. She started rubbing her ankles. 'I'll pop in and see you tomorrow if you don't mind.'

I got down to my room and there was some bread and cheese on a tray and a glass of milk. I felt very tired. I looked at the bed and thought, 'There's one thing – I do sleep. I sleep as if I were dead.'

It's funny when you feel as if you don't want anything more in your life except to sleep, or else to lie without moving. That's when you can hear time sliding past you, like water running.

2

Mrs Flower said, 'Would you mind, miss, coming and sitting downstairs, because we want to turn the room out properly.'

'All right,' I said. 'I'm going out this afternoon.'

I got up and dressed and took the Tube to Tottenham Court Road and went along Oxford Street. As I was passing the Richelieu Hotel a girl in a squirrel coat came out. Two men were with her.

'Hullo,' she said. I looked at her and said, 'Hullo, Laurie?'

'Just bumming around, Anna?' she said in a voice that was as hoarse as a crow's.

She introduced me to the two men. They were Americans. The big one was Carl – Carl Redman – and the other one's name was Adler. Joe, she called him. He was the younger, and very Jewish-looking. You would have known he was a Jew wherever you saw him, but I wasn't sure about Carl.

'Where have you sprung from?' Laurie said. 'Come along up to my flat and have a drink. I live just round the corner in Berners Street.'

'No,' I said, 'I can't today, Laurie.' I didn't want to talk to anybody. I felt too much like a ghost.

'Oh, come on,' she said. She took hold of my arm.

Carl said, 'Well, don't try to kidnap the girl, Laurie. If she doesn't want to come, leave her alone.' He had a calm way of talking, as if he were very sure of himself.

As soon as he said that I changed my mind. 'All right,' I said. 'I wasn't going anywhere in particular. Only I've been ill and I still feel a bit seedy.'

'This kid was with me last year in a show,' Laurie said. She began to laugh. 'My Lord, that was a show, too, wasn't it? I didn't go back with it, you know. There's nothing like that about me. I got a job in town, only the thing didn't run very long.'

Her flat was about half-way along Berners Street, on the second floor. We went upstairs into the sitting-room. There was a table covered with a red cloth in the middle, and a sofa, and flowered wall-paper. The whole place smelt of her scent.

She got whiskies-and-sodas for everybody. Carl and Joe were easy to talk to. You didn't feel they were getting ready to sneer at you behind your back, as you do with some men.

After a bit Carl said, 'At a quarter to nine tonight, then. Will you bring your friend along too?'

'Would you like to come, Anna?' Laurie said.

'Do come along if you'd like to,' Carl said.

'They're both staying at the Carlton,' Laurie told me. 'I met them in Frankfort. And I went to Paris too. My dear, I've been getting about a bit, I can tell you.'

She had hennaed her hair. It was cut short with a thick fringe. It suited her. But she had too much blue on her eyelids. Too much 'Overture and Beginners', I thought. She went on about how lucky she had been and what a lot of men with money she knew and what a good time she was having.

'D'you know,' she said, 'I never pay for a meal for myself – it's the rarest thing. For instance, these two – I said to them quite casually, like that, "When you come over to London, let me know. I'll show you round a bit," and if you please about three weeks ago they turned up. I've been showing them round, I can tell you. . . . I get along with men. I can do what I like with them. Sometimes I'm surprised myself. I expect it's because they feel I really like it and no kidding. But what's the matter with you? You don't look well. Why don't you finish your drink?'

I finished it, and then I found I was crying.

'What's up?' Laurie said. 'Come on, never say die.'

After a bit I said, 'There was a man I was mad about. He got sick of me and chucked me. I wish I were dead.'

'Are you going to have a baby or something?' she said. 'Oh, no.'

'Did he give you any money?'

'Of course he did,' I said, 'and I can get more any time I write to him. I'm going to write to him quite soon about it.' I said that because I didn't want to seem a fool and as if I had been utterly done in.

'Well,' Laurie said, 'I shouldn't wait too long if I were you – not too long. However, if it's like that it's not so bad. It might have been much worse.'

I said, 'It was when I wasn't expecting it to happen, you see – just when I wasn't expecting it. He went away and I worried like anything. But then he wrote to me. About how fond he was of me and so on and how much he wanted to see me, and I thought it was all right. And it wasn't.'

'It's always like that,' she said, looking down at the table. 'They always do it that way. Search me what the whole thing's about. When you start thinking about things the answer's a lemon. A lemon, that's what the answer is. ... But it's no use worrying. Why worry about a man who's well in bed with somebody else by this time? It's soppy. Think of it like that.'

She had another whisky and went on about being clever and putting money away, and her voice joined in with the smell of the room. 'There are all sorts of lives,' I thought.

'I bank half of everything I get,' she said. 'Even if I have to do without, I still bank half of everything I get, and there's no friend like that. . . . Never mind, you're a good little cow; you'll be all right. Come along and have a look at the flat.'

Her bedroom was small and very tidy. There were no photographs and no pictures. There was a huge bed and a long plait of hair on the dressing-table.

'I kept that,' she said. 'I pin it on sometimes when I wear nightgowns. Of course, in pyjamas I keep my own short hair. Why don't you cut your hair? You ought; it would suit you. Heaps of girls in Paris have their hair cut, and I bet they will here too sooner or later. And false eyelashes, my dear, sticking out yards – you should see them. They know what's what, I tell you. Are you coming tonight? Would you like to? I'm sure you'll go well with Carl because you look awfully young and he likes girls that look young. But he's a funny cuss. He only cares about gambling really. He's found a place in Clarges Street. He took me the other day – I won nearly twenty quid. He's got a business in Buenos Aires. Joe's his secretary.'

I said, 'I can't come in this dress. It's torn under the arm and awfully creased. Haven't you noticed? That's why I keep my coat on. I tore it like that last time I took it off.' It was my black velvet dress that I had on.

'I'll lend you a dress,' she said.

She sat down on the bed and yawned. 'Well, give us a kiss. I'm going to lie down for a bit. There's a gas-fire in the other bedroom if you'd like to go and have a rest.'

'I'd like a bath,' I said. 'Could I?'

'Ma,' she yelled out, 'turn on a bath for Miss Morgan.' Nobody answered.

'Now, what's she up to?'

We went into the kitchen. An old woman was sitting by the table, asleep, with her head in her arms.

'She's always doing this,' Laurie said. 'She's always going to sleep on me. I'd fire the old sod tomorrow only I know she'd never get another job.' She touched the old woman's shoulder gently. 'Go on, Ma, wake up. Turn a bath on and get some tea. And hurry for once in your life, for God's sake.'

The window of the bathroom was open and the soft, damp air from outside blew in on my face. There was a white bath-wrap on the chair. I put it on afterwards and went and lay down and the old woman brought me in some tea. I felt emptied-out and peaceful – like when you've had toothache and it stops for a bit, and you know quite well it's going to start again but just for a bit it's stopped.

3

We met Carl and Joe at Oddenino's. Melville Gideon was at the piano; he was singing rather well.

Carl talked to the waiter for a long time about what we were going to eat before he ordered it. We had Château Yquem to drink.

By the time we had finished dinner and were having liqueurs Laurie seemed a bit tight.

She said, 'Well, Carl, what do you think of my little pal? Don't you think I've found a nice girl for you?'

'A peach,' Carl said in a polite voice.

'I don't like the way English girls dress,' Joe said. 'American girls dress differently. I like their way of dressing better.'

''Ere, 'ere,' Laurie said, 'that'll do. Besides, she's got on one of my dresses if you want to know.'

'Ah,' Carl said, 'that's another story then.'

'Don't you like the dress, Carl, what's wrong with it?'

'Oh, I don't know,' Carl said. 'Anyway it doesn't matter so much.'

He put his hand on mine and smiled. He had very nice teeth. His nose looked as if it had been broken some time.

'Look out, you bloody fool, don't spill it,' Laurie said in a loud voice to the waiter, who was pouring out another liqueur for her.

Joe stopped talking and looked embarrassed.

'And the bill,' Carl said.

'Yes, l'addition, l'addition,' Laurie called out. 'I know a bit of every language in Europe – even Polish. Shall I say my bit of Polish?'

'The woman at the next table's looking at you in a very funny way,' Joe said.

'Well, the woman!' Laurie said. 'She's looking at me. Look, pretty creature, look! And she is a pretty creature too, isn't she? My God, she's got a face like an old hen's. I'll say my bit of Polish to her in a minute.'

'No, don't do that, Laurie,' Carl said.

'Well, why shouldn't I?' Laurie said. 'What right has a woman with a face like a hen's – and like a hen's behind too – to look at me like that?'

Joe started to laugh. He said, 'Oh, women. How you love each other, don't you?'

'Well, that's an original remark,' Carl said. 'We're all being very original.'

'Don't you ever talk at all?' he said to me. 'What do you think about the lady at the next table? She certainly doesn't look as if she loves us.'

I said, 'I think she's terrifying,' and they all laughed.

But I was thinking that it was terrifying – the way they look at you. So that you know that they would see you burnt alive without even turning their heads away; so that you know in yourself that they would watch you burning without even blinking once. Their glassy eyes that don't admit anything so definite as hate. Only just that underground hope that you'll be burnt alive, tortured, where they can have a peep. And slowly, slowly you feel the hate back starting ...

'Terrifying?' Laurie said. 'She doesn't terrify me. I'm not so easily terrified. I've got good strong peasant blood in me.'

'That's the first time I've heard an English girl boast about having peasant blood,' Joe said. 'They try to tell you they're descended from William the Conqueror or whatever his name was, as a rule.'

'There's only one Laurie,' Carl said.

'That's right,' Laurie said, 'and when I die there won't be another.'

I kept wondering whether I should be able to walk without staggering when we got up. 'You must seem all right,' I kept telling myself.

We got out of the restaurant.

I said, 'Just a minute.'

'It's through those curtains,' Laurie said.

I stayed a long time in the ladies' room. There was a chair and I sat down. The tune of the Robert E. Lee was going in my head.

After a while the woman said, 'Aren't you feeling well, miss?'

'Oh yes,' I said. 'I'm quite well, thank you.' I put a shilling into the plate on the table and went out.

'We thought you'd got drowned,' Laurie said.

In the taxi I asked, 'Did I seem drunk as we came out?'

'Of course you didn't,' Joe said. He was sitting between Laurie and myself, holding both our hands.

'But where's Carl?' I said.

Laurie said, 'Echo answers Where?'

'Carl asked me to say good night for him to you and to excuse him to you,' Joe said. 'But he had a very urgent telephone message. He's had to go back to the hotel.'

'Back to the hotel my eye,' Laurie said. 'I know where he's gone. He's gone to Clarges Street. I think it's too bad of him to walk off like that. It really is a bit rude.'

'Oh well, you know how Carl is,' Joe said. 'Besides, you've got me. What are you grumbling about?'

4

'Is this right?' Joe said. We got out of the taxi. Laurie put her arm through mine and we went into the hotel. There was a smell of cooking and RITZ-PLAZA in black letters on a dusty doormat.

A fat man came up. Joe spoke to him in German. He said something and then the man said something.

Joe said, 'He won't let us have one room, so I've taken two.'

'This way, please,' the man said.

We followed him upstairs into a big bedroom. It had dark-brown wallpaper and the fire was laid .The man took a box of matches out of his pocket and lit it.

The mantelpiece was very high and painted black. There were two huge dark-blue vases on it and a clock, stopped at ten minutes past three.

'My God,' Joe said, 'this place is kind of gloomy.'

'Lugubrious,' Laurie said. 'That's the word you mean

– lugubrious. It's all right. It'll look different when the fire burns up.'

'What a lot of long words she knows, doesn't she?' Joe said.

'Long words is my middle name,' Laurie said.

The man was still standing there, smiling.

'What'll you have to drink, Laurie?' Joe said.

'Just whisky-and-soda for me,' Laurie said. 'I'm going to stick to whisky-and-soda for the rest of the evening and not too much of it either.'

'Let's have a bottle of Black and White.' Joe said, 'and some soda.'

The man went out.

'It's bare,' Joe said. 'You don't go in for frills in this burg, do you?' He went on, talking about barbers' shops in London. He said they weren't comfortable, that they didn't know how to make you comfortable.

The man knocked at the door and brought in the whisky.

'Oh, go on,' Laurie said. 'London's not so bad. It has a certain gloomy charm when you get used to it, as a man I know said.'

'He's right about the gloom,' Joe said.

Laurie began to sing *Moonlight Bay*.

> 'You have stolen my heart,
> So don't go away.'

I said, 'I'll have a whisky-and-soda. Why are you leaving me out?'

I drank half the glass and then I felt very giddy. I said, 'I'm going to lie down. I feel so damned giddy.'

I lay down. As long as I kept my eyes open it wasn't so bad.

Laurie said, 'You ought to take that dress off then. You're creasing it all up.'

'That would be a pity,' I said.

It was a pink dress, with silver bits and pieces dangling here and there.

She came over and helped me to undo it. She seemed very tall and her face enormous. I could see all the lines in it, and the powder, trying to fill up the lines, and just where her lipstick stopped and her lips began. It looked like a clown's face, so that I wanted to laugh at it. She was pretty, but her hands were short and fat with wide, flat, very red nails.

Joe lit a cigarette and crossed his legs and watched us. He was like somebody sitting in the stalls, waiting for the curtain to go up. When it was all over he was ready to clap and say, 'That was well done,' or to hiss and say, 'That was badly done' – as the case might be.

'I feel awfully sick,' I said. 'I must keep still for a bit.'

'Oh, don't go and be sick,' Laurie said. 'Pull yourself to pieces.'

'Well, just a minute,' I said.

I felt very cold. I pulled the eiderdown over my shoulders and shut my eyes. The bed sank under me. I opened them again.

They were sitting near the fire, laughing. Their black shadows on the wall were laughing too.

'How old is she?' Joe said.

'She's only a kid,' Laurie said. She coughed and then she said, 'She's not seventeen.'

'Yes – and the rest,' Joe said.

'Well, she's not a day older than nineteen, anyway,' Laurie said. 'Where do you see the wrinkles? Don't you like her?'

'She's all right,' Joe said, 'but I liked that other kid – the dark one.'

'Who? Renée?' Laurie said. 'I don't know what's happened to her. I haven't seen her since that evening.'

Joe came over to the bed. He took hold of my hand and stroked it.

I said, 'I know what you're going to say. You're going

to say it's cold and clammy. Well, it's because I was born in the West Indies and I'm always like that.'

'Oh, were you?' Joe said. He sat on the bed. 'I know, I know. Trinidad, Cuba, Jamaica – why, I've spent years there.' He winked at Laurie.

'No,' I said, 'a little one.'

'But I know the little ones too,' Joe said. 'The little one, the big ones, the whole lot.'

'Oh, do you?' I said, sitting up.

'Yes, of course I do,' Joe said. He winked at Laurie again. 'Why, I knew your father – a great pal of mine. Old Taffy Morgan. He was a fine old boy, and didn't he lift the elbow too.'

'You're a liar,' I said. 'You didn't know my father. Because my real name isn't Morgan and I'll never tell you my real name and I was born in Manchester and I'll never tell you anything real about myself. Everything that I tell you about myself is a lie, so now then.'

He said, 'Well, wasn't his name Taffy? Was it Patrick, perhaps?'

'Oh, go to hell,' I said. 'And get off this bed. You get on my nerves.'

'Hey,' Laurie said, 'what's the matter with you? Are you tight, or what?'

'I was only joking,' Joe said. 'I didn't mean to hurt your feelings, kid.'

I got out of bed. I was still very giddy.

'Well,' Laurie said, 'what's the matter now?'

'You both get on my nerves, if you want to know,' I said. 'If you could see yourselves when you're laughing you wouldn't laugh so much.'

'You're damned good company, aren't you?' Laurie said. 'What d'you want to ask me to take you out for, if you're going to behave like this?'

I said, 'Well, where's my dress? I'm going home. I'm sick of your damned party.'

'I like that,' Laurie said. 'If you think you're going to walk off with my clothes you've got another guess coming.'

The dress was hanging over the end of the bed. I took hold of it, but she hung on to it. We both pulled. Joe started to laugh.

'If you tear my dress,' Laurie said, 'I'll knock your block off.'

I said, 'Try it. Just try it. And you'll get the surprise of your life.'

'Oh, leave her alone, Laurie. She's drunk,' Joe said. 'You lie down and go to sleep, kid. You'll feel better to-morrow morning. Nobody's going to trouble you.'

'I won't lie down in here,' I said.

'All right,' Joe said, making a movement with his chin. 'There's a room opposite – just opposite. You go in there.'

Laurie didn't say anything. She kept the dress over her arm.

Joe got up and opened the door. He said, 'There you are – the room just opposite, see.'

'And try not to be sick on the floor,' Laurie said. 'There's a lavatory at the end of the passage.'

'Oh, one word to you,' I said.

'And the same to you and many of them,' she said in a mechanical voice. Like the kids at home when they used to answer questions in the catechism. 'Who made you?' 'God made me.' 'Why did God make you?' And so on.

The other room was much smaller. There was no fire. There was no key in the lock. I lay down.

There were only a sheet and a thin counterpane on the bed. It was as cold as being in the street.

I thought, 'Well, what a night! My God, what an idiotic night!'

There was a spot on the ceiling. I looked at it and it became two spots. The two spots moved very rapidly, one away from the other. When they were about six inches apart they remained stationary and grew larger. Two black eyes were staring at me. I stared back at them. Then I had to blink and the whole business began all over again.

There was Joe by the bed, saying, 'Don't be mad with me. I was only teasing you.'

'I'm not,' I said, but when he began to kiss me I said, 'No, don't.'

'Why not?' he said.

'Some other night,' I said. 'Ça sera pour un autre soir.' (A girl in a book said that. Some girl in some book. Ça sera pour un autre soir.)

He didn't say anything for a bit and then he said, 'Why do you go around with Laurie? Don't you know she's a tart?'

'Well,' I said, 'why shouldn't she be a tart? It's just as good as anything else, as far as I can see.'

'I don't get you,' he said. 'You're quaint, as they say over here.'

'Oh God,' I said, 'do leave me alone, do leave me alone.'

Something came out from my heart into my throat and then into my eyes.

Joe said, 'Don't do that, don't cry. D'you know, kid, I like you. I thought I didn't, but I do. I'd better go and get something to put over you. This room's as cold as hell.'

'Is Laurie vexed?' I said.

'She'll get over it,' he said.

I opened my eyes, and he was putting an eiderdown over me, and my coat. I went to sleep again.

Somebody knocked at the door. I got up and there was a can of hot water outside. I poured it into the basin and started washing my face. While I was washing Laurie walked in with the dress over her arm.

She said, 'Come on, let's get out of this.'

I put the dress on. I looked pretty awful, I thought.

'Where's Joe?' I said.

'He's gone,' Laurie said. 'He left half an hour ago. What did you imagine – that he'd walk out arm in arm with us? He asked me to say good-bye to you. Come on.'

I was thinking, 'Well, what a night! My God, what a night!'

We got out into the street. All the houses seemed to be hotels. The Bellevue, the Welcome, the Cornwall, the Sandringham, the Berkeley, the Waverley. ... All the way up. And, of course, spiked railings. It was a fine day. The mist was blue instead of grey.

A policeman standing near by stared at us. He was a big man with a small, rosy face. His helmet seemed enormous on the top of his small face.

I said, 'I shall have to come back with you to get my dress. I'm sorry.'

'Well, I didn't say you couldn't, did I?' Laurie said.

She stopped a taxi. When it had started she said, 'Swine!'

'D'you mean me?' I said.

She said, 'Don't be a fool. I meant the bloody bobby.'

'Oh, I thought you meant me.'

'What you do doesn't concern me,' Laurie said. 'I think you're a bit of a fool, that's all. And I think you'll never get on, because you don't know how to take people. After all, to say you'll come out with somebody and then to get tight and start a row about nothing at all isn't a way to behave. And besides, you always look half-asleep and people don't like that. But it's not my business.'

We got to Berners Street and went upstairs. The old woman came to the door to meet us.

'Shall I get breakfast, miss?'

'Yes,' Laurie said, 'and turn a bath on, and hurry up.'

I stood in the passage. She went into the bedroom and brought my dress out.

'Here's your dress,' she said. 'And for God's sake don't look like that. Come on and have something to eat.'

She kissed me all of a sudden.

'Oh, come on,' she said. 'I'm a good old cow really. You know I'm fond of you. To tell you the truth I was a bit screwed last night too. You can pretend to be a virgin for the rest of your life as far as I'm concerned; I don't care. What's it got to do with me?'

'Don't start a speech,' she said, 'I've got a splitting headache. Have a heart.'

It was the first fine day for weeks. The old woman spread a white cloth on the table in the sitting-room and the sun shone in on it. Then she went into the kitchen and started to fry bacon. There was the smell of the bacon and the sound of the water running into the bath. And nothing else. My head felt empty.

5

It was four o'clock when I left the flat. I walked along Oxford Street, thinking about my room in Camden Town and that I didn't want to go back to it. There was a black velvet dress in a shop-window, with the skirt slit up so that you could see the light stocking. A girl could look lovely in that, like a doll or a flower. Another dress, with fur round the neck, reminded me of the one that Laurie had worn. Her neck coming out of the fur was a pale-gold colour, very slim and strong-looking.

The clothes of most of the women who passed were like caricatures of the clothes in the shop-windows, but when they stopped to look you saw that their eyes were fixed on the future. 'If I could buy this, then of course I'd be quite different.' Keep hope alive and you can do anything, and that's the way the world goes round, that's the way they keep the world rolling. So much hope for each person. And damned cleverly done too. But what happens if you don't hope any more, if your back's broken? What happens then?

'I can't stand here staring at these dresses for ever,' I thought. I turned round and there was a taxi going past slowly. The driver looked at me and I stopped him and said, '227, Bird Street.'

There were two bells. I rang the lower one. Nobody came, but when I pushed the door it opened.

There was a passage with a short flight of stairs and a door on the left-hand side. I went outside and rang again. The door on the left opened and an elderly man wearing pince-nez said, 'Well, Miss?'

The room he had come out of was an office. There was a filing-cabinet, and a table with a typewriter and a lot of letters, and two chairs.

I said, 'I wanted to see Miss Ethel Matthews. I thought she lived here.'

'Upstairs,' the man said. 'You rang the wrong bell.'

'I'm sorry.'

'This is the fourth time today,' he said. 'Will you kind-ly tell Miss Matthews that I object to being disturbed like this?' He stood at the door and talked rather loudly. 'I've got other things to do. I can't be answering her bell all day long.'

I saw Ethel standing at the bend in the staircase. She peered down at me.

'Oh, it's you, is it?' she said.

'Hullo,' I said. I went up.

She was wearing a white overall with the sleeves rolled up. Her hair was tidy. She looked much nicer than I had remembered her.

She said, 'What was Denby gassing about?'

'He was saying that I'd rung the wrong bell.'

'I must have a plate put up,' she said. 'He's such a swine. Come on in; I'm just having tea.'

The sitting-room looked out on Bird Street. There was

a gas-stove with a bowl of water in front of it. The two armchairs had glazed chintz covers with a pattern of small rosebuds. There was a very high divan in one corner, with a rug over it. And a piano. The wallpaper was white, with stripes.

'I'll get another cup,' she said.

We drank the tea.

'Who's the man downstairs?' I said.

'That's the owner,' she said. 'He's got the office there. Well, he calls it his office; he says he's a stamp-dealer. I believe he just comes and sits there. He's out most of the time. An old devil, he is. ... I've got this floor and the third floor. There's nothing like glazed chintz for making a room look cheerful, is there? It's small, of course, but the dining-room next door is big and my bedroom's a fair size, too.'

In the dining-room there were the *Cries of London* on the walls and a plate of fruit on the sideboard.

Ethel said, 'You thought I was pretending, didn't you? You didn't believe I had such a nice flat? Come and see the room I told you about.'

We went up to the floor above.

'It's what I call dainty,' Ethel said, 'though I say it myself. And I could have a gas-fire put in.'

The furniture was painted white. It was a big room, but rather dark because the blinds were pulled half-way down. I looked out of the window at a barrel-organ. It was playing *Moonlight Bay*.

'Sit down,' she said, patting the bed. 'You look tired.'

'Yes,' I said, 'I am a bit.'

She said, 'I want somebody to share the flat and help me with my business, as I told you. It's all U.P. with that girl I spoke about. I didn't want her, but I'm sure we'd get on all right. Why don't you make up your mind? Isn't this better than that room in Camden Town?'

I said, 'Yes, the room's fine. It's a very nice room. But

you said you wanted somebody to put twenty-five quid into your business. I haven't got twenty-five quid.'

'Oh, twenty-five quid,' she said. 'What about this? We'll say eight quid a month. That'll be for the room and food. And I'll teach you to do manicure and you can get half of what you make out of that. Of course, you'll have to help me out with the house-work and receive the patients and so on. What about it? You don't think eight quid's too much for this lovely room, do you? And the whole flat as bright and clean as anything you'd find any-where.'

'No,' I said, 'I think it's very cheap.'

'Go on, make up your mind. Sometimes when you do things on the spur of the moment it brings you luck. It changes your luck. Haven't you ever noticed? Can you manage eight quid?'

'Yes, I can manage that.'

'There you are then. That's settled,' Ethel said. 'Only I shall have to ask you to give it to me in advance, because I've had a lot of expenses doing up this place. You can see that, can't you? It cost me pretty nearly six quid to do up this room alone. Well, but it's a lovely room now. And a bathroom next door and everything. You should have seen the state it was in when I came.'

'All right,' I said, 'but it doesn't leave me with much.'

'Don't you worry about that,' Ethel said. 'It's the first few weeks that are going to be difficult in a thing like this. I won't ask you to pay in advance next month. When once I get my business going you'll see it'll be all right about money. You'll be able to make quite a bit.'

We went downstairs. I took two five-pound notes out of my bag and gave her one and three sovereigns and put the other note back.

She said, 'Of course, when I said I'd do it for eight quid I was making it as cheap as possible. God knows if I shall be able to manage. We'll have to see how things go. However, it'll be all right for a couple of weeks anyway with this.'

'I'll have to go to Camden Town and get my things and settle up,' I said.

I got back to Bird Street and told Ethel I wanted to go to bed. My back hurt.

'I'll bring you something to eat,' she said.

I was lying down thinking about money and that I had only three pounds left when she came in with bread and cheese and a bottle of Guinness. She sat by my side while I ate and began to tell me how respectable she was.

'It's all straight and above-board with me,' she said. 'I'm the best masseuse in London. You couldn't learn from anybody better than me. It really is a chance for you. Of course, if you can introduce some clients of your own it'll be all the better for both of us.'

'Well,' I said, 'I don't know. I can't think of a soul at present – not a soul.'

'You're a bit tired tonight,' she said. 'I can see that. You'd better have a good rest. I'll put the alarm to eight o'clock. You won't mind getting breakfast, will you? The kitchen's on this floor, so it'll be easy for you. You don't mind?'

'No,' I said. 'All right.'

She went out. And I lay there and thought.

... She'll smile and put the tray down and I'll say Francine I've had such an awful dream – it was only a dream she'll say – and on the tray the blue cup and saucer and the silver teapot so I'd know for certain that it had started again my lovely life – like a five-finger exercise played very slowly on the piano like a garden with a high wall round it – and every now and again thinking I only dreamt it it never happened ...

Part Three

I

There were the *Cries of London* in the dining-room. I remember the way they hung, and the bowl of water in
front of the gas-fire, and always a plate of oranges in the
middle of the table, and two armchairs with chintz
cushions – a different pattern from the chintz in the sitting-room – and Ethel talking about how respectable
she was. 'If I were to tell you all I know about some of the
places that advertise massage. That Madame Fernande,
for instance – well, the things I've heard about her and
the girls she's got at her place. And how she manages to do
it without getting into trouble I don't know. I expect it
costs her something.'

The window would be open because it was warm that
November, but the blind half-way down at the top. When
the bell rang I would go downstairs and bring the man up
and say to Ethel, 'He's in the other room.' And after a
while she would come back and start again. 'Did I tell
you about what happened last week? Well, it just shows
you. The day after I'd put in my advertisement there were
detectives calling and wanting to see my references and
my certificates. I showed them some references, and some
certificates too. I was wild. Treating me as if I was a dirty
foreigner.'

She used to wear a white overall. Her face was rather
red and her nose turned-up with wide nostrils.

She said – that must have been the first day – 'About
manicure, the main thing is to have a nice set of manicure
things. I'll lend you those. You get them all spread out

119

nicely on the table with a white cloth and a bowl of soapy hot water and you push one of the armchairs forward and smile and say, "Please sit down." And then you say, "Do you mind?" and you put his hand into a bowl of hot water. It's awfully easy. Don't be silly, anybody can do it. You can practise on me if you like. And you can ask five bob. You might even be able to get ten bob. Use your judgement.'

'Of course,' she said, 'you must be a bit nice to them.'

'Why not ten bob?' she said. 'That's all right. Everybody's got their living to earn and if people do things thinking that they're going to get something that they don't get, what's it matter to you or me or anybody else? You let them talk. You can take it from me that when it comes to it they're all so damned afraid of a scene that they're off like a streak of lightning at the slightest ...'

That's what I can remember best – Ethel talking and the clock ticking. And her voice when she was telling me about Madame Fernande or about her father, who had a chemist's shop, and that she was really a lady. A lady – some words have a long, thin neck that you'd like to strangle. And her different voice when she said, 'A manicure, dear.'

There were never any scenes. There was nothing to make scenes about. But I stopped going out; I stopped wanting to go out. That happens very easily. It's as if you had always done that – lived in a few rooms and gone from one to the other. The light is a different colour every hour and the shadows fall differently and make different patterns. You feel peaceful, but when you try to think it's as if you're face to face with a high, dark wall. Really all you want is night, and to lie in the dark and pull the sheet over your head and sleep, and before you know where you are it is night – that's one good thing. You pull the sheet over your head and think, 'He got sick of me,' and 'Never, not ever, never.' And then you go to sleep.

You sleep very quickly when you are like that and you don't dream either. It's as if you were dead.

'Oh, shut up about being tired,' she would say. 'You were born tired. I'm tired too. We're all tired.'

I had been nearly three weeks in Bird Street before I saw Laurie again. She came to lunch.

'Now, that's the sort of girl I should want if I were a man,' Ethel said. 'Look at the way she walks. Look at the way she wears her clothes. My God, that's what I call smart.'

'She's a funny old cow,' Laurie said to me afterwards up in my room. 'But she seems very affable – very affable indeed. Is she really teaching you to do manicure? Do you get many people to manicure?'

'I've had four or five,' I said.

'What, to manicure?'

'Yes, to manicure,' I said. 'One of them did ask me to take him upstairs, but when I said No he went off like a shot. He was a bit frightened all the time, you could tell that.'

Laurie laughed. She said, 'I bet the old girl wasn't pleased. I bet you that wasn't her idea at all.'

A car hooted outside and she looked out of the window and made signs. She called out, 'I'll be down in a minute.'

'There they are, my two specimens. Why don't you come out with us for a blow?' she said. 'It'll cheer you up. The old girl won't mind, will she?'

'No, I don't think so. Why should she?'

'Come on then,' Laurie said.

I kept thinking, 'I'm all right. I still like going fast in a car and eating and drinking and hot baths. I'm quite all right.'

'My shoe's undone,' Laurie said. When the man did it up his hands were trembling. ('I can always make people crazy about me.')

The long shadows of the trees, like skeletons, and others like spiders, and others like octopuses. 'I'm quite all right; I'm quite all right. Of course, everything will be all right. I've only got to pull myself together and make a plan.' ('Have you heard the one about ...')

It was one of those days when you can see the ghosts of all the other lovely days. You drink a bit and watch the ghosts of all the lovely days that have ever been from behind a glass. ('Yes, that's not a bad one, but have you heard the one ...')

'If you'd let me know you were going to be so late I'd have given you a key,' Ethel said. 'I didn't want to have to sit up half the night to let you in.'

'We went to supper at Romano's,' I said. 'That's why I'm so late.'

'Well, I hope you enjoyed yourself,' she said. But I knew from the way she looked at me that she had started to hate me. I knew she was going to make a row sooner or later.

Nobody came all the next morning.

'I'm fed up,' Ethel said, 'I'm fed up with the whole damned business. There's nobody coming till five.'

She poured herself out another whisky-and-soda. Then she had another and then she said, 'A fourth for luck,' and filled the glass up and took it into the sitting-room.

I heard her talking to herself. She did that sometimes. 'Brutes and idiots, idiots and brutes,' she would say. 'If it's not brutes it's idiots and if it's not idiots it's brutes.' And 'Oh God, God, God, God, God.'

At about five o'clock somebody rang, and I went down and brought him up. Then she knocked on the wall and called out for hot water. I got the kettle and put it outside the sitting-room door.

The man had been there for about twenty minutes when I heard the crack of wood breaking and he started to swear at the top of his voice. Ethel knocked again.

'Am I to come in?' I said at the door.

'Yes,' she said, 'come in.'

I went in. The massage couch had collapsed at one end and the basin was upset. There was water all over the floor. The man had a blanket wrapped round him. He was hopping around on one leg, holding the other foot, and swearing. He looked very thin and small. He had grey hair; I didn't notice his face.

'There's been an accident,' Ethel said. 'One of the legs of the couch has given way. Get a cloth or the water will drip through on Denby's head. ... I'm ever so sorry. Does your foot hurt?'

'D'you think I can stand in boiling water and not get hurt, you damned fool?' the man said.

While I was mopping up the water he sat on the piano-stool playing with one finger. But his foot kept jerking up and down, as a thing does when it has been hurt. Long after you have stopped thinking about it, it keeps jerking up and down.

As soon as I got out of the room I began to laugh, and then I couldn't stop. It's like that when you haven't laughed for a long time.

I heard him going downstairs and Ethel came in.

'This is a bit of a change – you laughing,' she said.

'Well,' I said, 'it was damned funny. It was a hymn he was playing, did you hear?'

'One end of the couch gave way,' she said, 'and instead of lying still the silly fool must jump up and put his foot into the basin of hot water. Couldn't he look where he was putting his blasted foot? It's your fault. What did you want to bring scalding water for?'

'Cheer up,' I said. 'It was really rather funny.' I knew she was getting ready to go for me, but I couldn't stop laughing.

'You're a nice one to tell anybody to cheer up,' she said. 'Who are you laughing at? Look here, I'll tell you something. You can clear out. You're no good; I don't want you here.'

'I wanted a smart girl,' she said, 'who'd be a bit nice to people and the way you seemed I thought you were the sort of kid who'd take the trouble to be nice to people and make a few friends and so on and try to make the place go. And as a matter of fact you're enough to drive anybody crazy with that potty look of yours. And then you clear off with your friends and you don't even ask me to come with you. Well, clear out and stay out. I don't want you here, you're no use. I know what you're going to say. You're going to say that you paid for a month, but do you know what it cost me to put in the gas-fire because you said you couldn't stand your bedroom without it, of all the damned nonsense? And always going on about being tired and it's being dark and cold and this, that and the other. What d'you want to stay here for, if you don't like it? Who wants you here anyway? Why don't you clear out?'

'I can't swim well enough, that's one reason,' I said.

'Christ,' she said, 'you're a funny turn, aren't you? Well, anyway, I haven't got any money to give you back, so it's no use expecting any.'

'All right,' I said, 'you can keep the money. There's lots more where that came from. Keep the change.'

'Keep what change?' she said. 'Who are you insulting?'

She was standing with her back to the door so that I couldn't get by.

'The thing about you,' she said, 'is that you're half potty. You're not all there; you're a half-potty bastard. You're not all there; that's what's the matter with you. Anybody's only got to look at you to see that.'

I said, 'All right. Well, get out of the way and let me pass.' But she collapsed on the floor and lay with her head and her back against the door and started to cry. I had never seen anybody cry like that. And all the time she went on talking.

'You went out with your pals and enjoyed yourself and you didn't even ask me. Wasn't I good enough to come?'

'But it's always the same thing. You didn't even ask me,' she said. 'And oh God, what a life I've had. Trying to keep up and everybody else trying to push you down and everybody lying and pretending and you knowing it. And then they down you for doing the same things as they do.'

'D'you know how old I am?' she said. 'If I can't get hold of some money in the next few years, what's going to become of me? Will you tell me that? You wait a bit and you'll see. It'll happen to you too. One day you'll see. You wait, you wait a bit.'

I watched her shoulders shaking. A fly was buzzing round me. I couldn't think of anything, except that it was December and too late for flies, or too soon, or something, and where did it come from?

'I'm always alone,' she said. 'It's awful to be always alone, awful, awful.'

'Never mind, cheer up,' I said.

She started looking for her handkerchief, but she didn't seem to have one. I gave her mine.

'Look here, kid, I didn't mean a word I said. Where are you going? Don't go, for God's sake. I can't stick it any longer. Please don't go. I beg you don't go. I can't stand being alone any longer. If you leave me I swear I'll turn the gas on.'

'I'll come back,' I said. 'I'm only going for a walk.'

'If you're not back in an hour,' she said, 'I'll turn the gas on and you'll have murdered me.'

I walked along imagining that I was going to his house, and the look of the street, and ringing the bell. 'You're late,' perhaps he'd say, 'I expected you before.'

Then I thought, 'If I went to that hotel in Berners

Street. I've got just about enough money on me to pay. They'd say, of course, that they hadn't got a room if you went in without any luggage. With the hotel half-empty they'd still say that they hadn't got a room.' I could imagine so well the girl at the desk saying it that I had to begin to laugh again. The damned way they look at you, and their damned voices, like high, smooth, unclimbable walls all round you, closing in on you. And nothing to be done about it, either. The answer's a lemon, as Laurie says. The damned way they look at you and their damned voices and the answer's a lemon as Laurie says.

I had on the jade bracelet that Walter had given me, and I slid it down over my hand. It felt warm and comforting against my hand and I gripped it and looked at it but I couldn't remember the word.

Thinking, 'Everybody says that if you start being afraid of people they see it and you're done for. Besides, it's all imagination.' I argued it out with myself quite solemnly, whether it was imagination or not that people are cruel. And I was holding my bracelet like that, slipped down over my hand. It felt warm and comforting because I knew I could hit somebody pretty hard with it. And I remembered the word. Knuckle-duster.

A man spoke to me out of the side of his mouth, like they do, but he went on quickly, before I could hit him. I went after him, meaning to hit him, but he walked too quickly, and a policeman at the corner of the street stared at me like a damned baboon — a fair baboon, too, worse than a dark one every time. (What happened to me then? Something happened to me then?)

I thought, 'You're not going to cry in the middle of the street, are you?' I got into a bus and went back to Bird Street.

When I opened the door Ethel called out, 'Oh, there you are, kid. I was awfully worried about you. Come and have some supper.'

She had brushed her hair and put on her black dress with a white collar. She looked quite all right – in fact, better than usual. I found out later that whenever she raved she always looked better than usual afterwards, fresher and younger.

'No, I don't want anything to eat,' I said.

'I'm sorry I went for you like that,' she said. 'I can't say more than that, can I?'

'It's all right,' I said. I only wanted to get upstairs and pull the sheet over my head and sleep.

'Nobody can do any more than say they're sorry,' she said.

The white furniture, and over the bed the picture of the dog sitting up begging – *Loyal Heart*. I got into bed and lay there looking at it and thinking of that picture advertising the Biscuits Like Mother Makes, as Fresh in the Tropics as in the Motherland, Packed in Airtight Tins, which they stuck up on a hoarding at the end of Market Street.

There was a little girl in a pink dress eating a large yellow biscuit studded with currants – what they called a squashed-fly biscuit – and a little boy in a sailor-suit, trundling a hoop, looking back over his shoulder at the little girl. There was a tidy green tree and a shiny pale-blue sky, so close that if the little girl had stretched her arm up she could have touched it. (God is always near us. So cosy.) And a high, dark wall behind the little girl.

Underneath the picture was written:

> The past is dear,
> The future clear,
> And, best of all, the present.

But it was the wall that mattered.

And that used to be my idea of what England was like.

'And it is like that, too,' I thought.

2

I didn't get up when the alarm went next morning. Ethel came in to see what was wrong.

I said, 'I want to stay in bed a bit today. I've got a headache.'

'Poor kid,' she said, blinking at me. 'You don't look well and that's a fact. I'll bring you up some breakfast.'

She had two voices – the soft one and the other one.

'Thanks,' I said. 'Just some tea – not anything to eat.'

I had to put the light on to see to pour the tea out.

'It's cold and there's an awful fog,' she said.

When I put the light out again the room was dark, and warm so long as I kept my hands under the blankets. I hadn't got a headache. I was all right really – only damned tired, worse than usual.

I kept telling myself, 'You've got to think of something. You can't stay here. You've got to make a plan.' But instead I started counting all the towns I had been to, the first winter I was on tour – Wigan, Blackburn, Bury, Oldham, Leeds, Halifax, Huddersfield, Southport. ... I counted up to fifteen and then slid off into thinking of all the bedrooms I had slept in and how exactly alike they were, bedrooms on tour. Always a high, dark wardrobe and something dirty red in the room; and through the window the feeling of a small street would come in. And the breakfast-tray dumped down on the bed, two plates with a bit of curled-up bacon on each. And if the landlady smiled or said 'Good morning' Maudie would say, 'She's very smarmy. What's the matter with her? I bet she puts that down on the bill. For saying Good Morning, half a crown.'

And then I tried to remember the road that leads to Constance Estate. It's funny how well you can remember when you lie in the dark with your arm over your forehead. Two eyes open inside your head. The sandbox tree outside the door at home and the horse waiting with his bridle over the hook that was fixed in the tree. And the sweat rolling down Joseph's face when he helped me to mount and the tear in my habit-skirt. And mounting, and then the bridge and the sound of the horse's hoofs on the wooden planks, and then the savannah. And then there is New Town, and just beyond New Town the big mango tree. It was just past there that I fell off the mule when I was a kid and it seemed such a long time before I hit the ground. The road goes along by the sea. The coconut palms lean crookedly down to the water. (Francine says that if you wash your face in fresh coconut-water every day you are always young and unwrinkled, however long you live.) You ride in a sort of dream, the saddle creaks sometimes, and you smell the sea and the good smell of the horse. And then – wait a minute. Then do you turn to the right or the left? To the left, of course. You turn to the left and the sea is at your back, and the road goes zigzag upwards. The feeling of the hills comes to you – cool and hot at the same time. Everything is green, everywhere things are growing. There is never one moment of stillness – always something buzzing. And then dark cliffs and ravines and the smell of rotten leaves and damp. That's how the road to Constance is – green, and the smell of green, and then the smell of water and dark earth and rotting leaves and damp. There's a bird called a Mountain Whistler, that calls out on one note, very high-up and sweet and piercing. You ford little rivers. The noise the horse's hoofs make when he picks them up and puts them down in the water. When you see the sea again it's far below you. It took three hours to get to Constance Estate. It was as long as a life sometimes. I was nearly twelve before I rode it by myself. There were bits in the road that I was afraid of. The turning where you came very suddenly out of the sun into the shadow; and the shadow was always the same shape. And the place where the woman with yaws spoke to me. I suppose she was begging but I couldn't understand because her nose and mouth were eaten away; it seemed as though she were laughing at me. I was frightened; I kept on looking backwards to see if she was following me, but when the horse came to the next ford and I saw clear water I thought I had forgotten about her. And now – there she is.

When Ethel brought me in something to eat at midday I pretended to be asleep. Then I did go to sleep.

The next time she came in she said, 'Listen. Two friends of Laurie's are downstairs, a Mr Redman and a Mr Adler. They've asked for you. Go on, go down, it'll cheer you up.'

She put the light on. It was a quarter to six. The tune of *Camptown Racecourse* was going in my head – I suppose I had been dreaming about it. I dressed and went down. Carl and Joe were in the sitting-room, and Ethel wreathed in smiles. I had never seen her look so good-tempered.

'Hullo, Anna,' Joe said, 'how have you been getting on?'

'I've been looking forward to meeting you again, Miss Morgan,' Carl said, in a formal voice.

Ethel smirked and said to Carl, 'Here she is. You wanted a manicure. She's a very good manicurist.'

I took him into the dining-room and got the table and put the armchair close to the fire. I started to file his nails, but my hands were trembling and the file kept slipping.

The third time it happened he began to laugh.

I said, 'I'm sorry, but I've not had a lot of practice at this.'

'I can see that,' he said.

'Ask Ethel to do it,' I said. 'She's really very good. I'll go and call her.'

I got up.

'Oh, don't worry about the manicure,' he said. 'I only wanted to talk to you.'

I sat down again. My mouth smiled at him.

He said, 'I was really sorry the other night about having to go away. I've been meaning to come and see you ever since, especially as I've heard such a lot about you from Laurie.'

He had brown eyes, rather close together. He wasn't nervous or hesitating. He was solid. I kept wanting to ask him, 'Was your nose ever broken?'

He said, 'Laurie's told me all about you.'

'Oh, has she?' I said.

'She likes you. She likes you a lot.'

'D'you think so?' I said.

'Well, she talks as though she does. And this one here – does she like you a lot too?'

'No, this one doesn't like me at all,' I said.

'That's too bad,' he said, 'that's too bad. And so she does the massage and you the manicure? Well, well, well.'

When he kissed me he said, 'You don't take ether, do you?'

'No,' I said, 'that's a face-lotion I use. It has ether in it.'

'Oh, that's it,' he said. 'You know, you mustn't be mad with me, but you look a bit as if you took something. Your eyes look like it.'

'No,' I said, 'I don't take ether. I never thought of it. I must try it sometime.'

He took my hand in both of his and warmed it.

'Cold,' he said, 'cold.' (Cold – cold as truth, cold as life. No, nothing can be as cold as life.)

He said, 'That guy Laurie says you were with – it doesn't look to me as if he was very nice to you.'

'He was. He was very nice,' I said.

He shook his head and said, 'Now, what have they

been doing to you?' in that voice which is just part of it. When he touched me I knew that he was quite sure I would. I thought, 'All right then, I will.' I was surprised at myself in a way and in another way I wasn't surprised. I think anything could have happened that day and I wouldn't have been really surprised. 'It's always on foggy days,' I thought.

He said, 'I'll tell you what we'll do. You go and get dressed and we'll go out and have some dinner somewhere. Not Joe – just you and I. Now I'll go and have a talk to Miss What's-her-name.'

All that evening I did everything to the tune of *Camptown Racecourse*. 'I'se gwine to ride all night, I'se gwine to ride all day . . .'

We went to Kettner's, and when we got back Ethel had gone out. There were two bottles of champagne on the table. He said, 'There you are. All done by kindness, as Laurie would say.'

Up in the bedroom I started singing:

> Oh, I bet my money on the bob-tailed nag,
> Somebody won on the bay,

and he said, 'It's "Somebody bet on the bay".'

I said, 'I'll sing it how I like it. Somebody won on the bay.'

He said, 'Nobody wins. Don't worry. Nobody wins.'

'Was your nose broken?'

'Yes, I'll tell you about it some time.'

The room still and dark and the lights from cars passing across the ceiling in long rays, and saying, 'Oh please, oh please, oh please . . .'

I didn't know when he went, because I was sleeping the way I sleep now – like a log.

3

Ethel turned the light on over the bed and woke me up.

'I thought you might like some breakfast. It's late – nearly eleven.'

'Thanks,' I said, 'but would you put the light out? I can see well enough.'

'It's all right between us now, kid, isn't it?'

I said, 'Yes, quite all right,' hoping she'd go out.

She was wearing her purple kimono with the white border and she walked up and down the room with little steps, jabbering.

'Because, I mean to say, I'm a good sport. I don't mind people enjoying themselves, and everybody isn't like that. If you went anywhere else you'd soon find out. But you'll be careful, won't you? Because of that Denby downstairs. He's an awful old cat. You can understand I don't want to give him any chance of turning me out of here after the money I've spent on the place.'

'Of course.'

'Did you have a good time? I bet you did. Redman's a nice man. He knows his way about, you can tell that. Oh, I bet he knows his way about. You know, kid, I've been thinking you'll want to go out more with your friends and not feel you've got to be in all day. I don't mind, but we may have to talk it over a bit about the rent.'

'All right,' I said. Then she did go out.

When she had gone I opened my handbag to get my handkerchief. Carl had put five quid inside. It was still foggy.

It was foggy for days after that and Carl didn't turn up again for a bit, or write or anything.

'I wonder what's happened to Redman,' Ethel said. 'He seems to have vanished.'

'I expect he's left London,' she'd say.

'Yes, probably.'

Then he telephoned and asked me to dine with him; and she cocked her eyes at me, looking surprised, looking suddenly respectful. That was when I started really hating her. I hated the way she smiled, I hated the way she'd say, 'Did you have a good time? Did you enjoy yourself?'

But I didn't see very much of her because I stayed late in bed in the mornings and took a long time dressing. The charwoman came an hour earlier and I didn't have to get up. If I brought Carl back to the flat after dinner she was usually out or in her bedroom. All done by kindness. ('And you do understand, kid, don't you? that under the circumstances two and a half guineas a week isn't too much to ask for this room? And really, you might say, the run of the whole flat. It's a nice flat to bring anybody to. It makes people think something of you when you bring them back to a place like this. People don't give you what you're worth – not in anything they don't. They give you what they think you're used to. That's where a nice flat comes in.')

Sometimes not being able to get over the feeling that it was a dream. The light and the sky and the shadows and the houses and the people – all parts of the dream, all fitting in and all against me. But there were other times when a fine day, or music, or looking in the glass and thinking I was pretty, made me start again imagining that there was nothing I couldn't do, nothing I couldn't become. Imagining God knows what. Imagining Carl would say, 'When I leave London, I'm going to take you with me.' And imagining it although his eyes had that look – this is just for while I'm here, and I hope you get me.

'I picked up a girl in London and she. . . . Last night I slept with a girl who. . . .' That was me.

Not 'girl' perhaps. Some other word, perhaps. Never mind.

'Are you staying much longer in London?'

'Why do you ask?'

'Nothing. It was just that I wondered.'

'Well, I may stay two or three weeks longer, I'm not sure. Joe's leaving next week; he's meeting his wife in Paris.'

'Oh, is Joe married?' I said. 'What a joke! I like Joe.' (He said, one day, 'What's the good of lying about it? We're all crabs in a basket. Have you ever seen crabs in a basket? One trying to get on top of the other. You want to survive, don't you?')

'Yes, he's married, all right. He's got two kids.'

'Are you married?'

'Yes,' he said. He looked vexed.

'Is your wife going to be in Paris too?'

'No.'

'Have you got any kids?'

'Yes,' he said after a while. 'A little girl.'

'Tell me about her,' I said. He didn't answer, so I said, 'Go on, tell me about her. Is she small, big, fair, dark? ...'

He said, 'Do you want to finish your coffee? Because I thought we might go to a show tonight and it's after nine o'clock.'

'For a change,' he said.

'Oh, I'd love a change, I'm all for that. I think the same thing all the time gets damned monotonous.'

'Oh, yes?' he said.

The streets looked like black oilcloth through the taxi-windows.

'You know, you're sweet when you laugh a lot,' he said. 'I like you best when you laugh a lot.'

'I'm damned nice. Don't you know I'm damned nice really?'

'Sure, I know.'

I said, 'I'll be nicer still when I've had a bit of practice.'
'I wonder,' he said.

He looked as if he were making up his mind not to see me again. But he came back several times after that. And he would say, 'Well, are you having a lot of practice?'

'You bet I am.'

'Well, you're in the right place to have some practice, I should say.'

The last time I went out with him he gave me fifteen quid. For several days after that I kept on planning to leave London. The names of all the places I could go to went round and round in my head. (This isn't the only place in the world; there are other places. You don't get so depressed when you think that.) And then I met Maudie coming out of Selfridge's and we went into a tea-shop. She didn't ask me many questions because she was full of a long story about an electrical engineer she had met who lived in Brondesbury and who was gone on her. She was sure she could get him to marry her if she could smarten herself up a bit.

She said, 'Isn't it awful losing a chance like that because you haven't got a little money? Because it is a chance. Sometimes you're sure, aren't you? But I'm so damned shabby and, you know, when you're shabby you can't do anything, you don't believe in yourself. And he notices clothes – he notices things like that. Fred, his name is. He said to me the other day, "If there's anything I notice about a girl it's her legs and her shoes." Well, my legs are all right, but look at my shoes. He's always saying things like that and it makes me feel awful. He's a bit strait-laced but that doesn't stop them from being particular. Viv was like that, too. Isn't it rotten when a thing like that falls through just because you haven't got a little cash? Oh God, I wish it could happen. I want it so to happen.'

When I asked her how much she wanted she said, 'I

could do a lot with eight pounds ten.' So I lent her eight pounds ten.

It's always like that with money. You never know where it goes to. You change a fiver and then it's gone.

4

Going up the stairs it was pretty bad but when we got into the bedroom and had drinks it was better.

'You've got a gramophone,' he said. 'Splendid! Have you got that perfectly lovely record of Bach's? It's a Concerto or something. Played by two violins – Kreisler and Zimbalist. I can't remember the exact name of it.'

He had a little, close-clipped moustache and one wrist was bandaged. Why was it bandaged? I don't know, I didn't ask. He didn't look as nice as I had thought when he spoke to me. I had gone by his voice. His eyes were a bit bleary.

'No, I haven't got anything of Bach's.'

I put on *Puppchen* and went on turning over the records.

'What's this one? *Connais-tu le Pays*? Do you know the country where the orange-tree flowers? Let's try that.'

'No, it gives me the pip,' I said.

I put on *Just a Little Love, a Little Kiss* and then *Puppchen* again. We started to dance and while we were dancing the dog in the picture over the bed stared down at us smugly. (Do you know the country? Of course, if you know the country it makes all the difference. The country where the orange-tree flowers?)

I said, 'I can't stand that damned dog any longer.'

I stopped dancing and took off my shoe and threw it at the picture. The glass smashed.

'I've wanted to do that for weeks,' I said.

He said, 'Good shot. But we're making rather a row, aren't we?'

I said, 'It's all right. We can make as much noise as we like. It doesn't matter. I should bloody well like to see her come up and say anything if I bloody well want to make a row.'

'Oh, quite,' he said, looking at me sideways.

We went on dancing. It started again.

I said, 'Let me go just a minute.'

'No; why?' he said, grinning at me.

'I feel awfully sick.'

The fool thought I was joking and held on to me.

I said, 'Do let me go,' but still he held on to me. I hit his bandaged wrist to make him let me go. It must have hurt him, because he started cursing me.

'What did you do that for, you little swine? You bitch.' And so on. And I couldn't stop to answer him back, either.

Like seasickness, only worse, and everything heaving up and down. And vomiting. And thinking, 'It can't be that, it can't be that. Oh, it can't be that. Pull yourself together; it can't be that. Didn't I always. . . . And besides it's never happened before. Why should it happen now?'

When I got back to the bedroom he had gone. Like a streak of lightning, as Ethel would have said. There was some glass on the floor. I swept it up into a piece of newspaper and piled the gramophone records one on top of the other. (Don't think of it, don't think of it. Because thinking of it makes it happen.)

I undressed and got into bed. Everything was still heaving up and down.

'Connais-tu le pays où fleurit l'oranger?'

. . . Miss Jackson used to sing that in a thin quavering voice and she used to sing By the Blue Alsatian Mountains I Watch and Wait Alway – Miss Jackson Colonel

Jackson's illegitimate daughter – yes illegitimate poor old thing but such a charming woman really and she speaks French so beautifully she really is worth what she charges for her lessons of course her mother was – it was very dark in her sitting-room the shabby palm-leaf fans and yellow photographs of men in uniform and through the window the leaves of the banana tree silken torn (tearing a banana-leaf was like tearing thick green silk but more easily and smoothly than you can tear silk) – Miss Jackson was very thin and straight and she always wore black – her dead-white face and her currant-black eyes glittering – yes you children can come and have your moonlight picnic in the garden but you mustn't throw things at Captain Cameron (Captain Cameron was her cat) – her voice always went so thin and small when she tried to speak loudly – calling out now now children no quarrelling no quarrelling frightening Captain Cameron and everything – the galvanized-iron fence at the end of her garden looked blue in the moonlight – it looked colder than anything I had ever seen or ever will see – and when she sang By the Blue Mountains.

The blue mountains – Morne Grand Bois one was called – and Morne Anglais Morne Collé Anglais Morne Trois Pitons Morne Rest – Morne Rest one was called – and Morne Diablotin its top always covered with clouds it's a high mountain five thousand feet with its top always veiled and Anne Chewett used to say that it's haunted and obeah – she had been in gaol for obeah (obeah-women who dig up dead people and cut their fingers off and go to gaol for it – it's hands that are obeah) – but can't they do damned funny things – Oh if you lived here you wouldn't take them so seriously as all that –

Obeah zombis soucriants – lying in the dark frightened of the dark frightened of soucriants that fly in through the window and suck your blood – they fan you to sleep with their wings and then they suck your blood – you know them in the day-time – they look like people but their eyes are red and staring and they're soucriants at night – looking in the glass and thinking sometimes my eyes look like a soucriant's eyes ...

The bed was heaving up and down and I lay there thinking, 'It can't be that. Pull yourself together. It can't be that. Didn't I always. . . . And all those things they say you can do. I know when it happened. The lamp over the bed had a blue shade. It was that one I went back with just after Carl left.' Counting back days and dates and thinking, 'No, I don't think it was that time. I think it was when ...'

Of course, as soon as a thing has happened it isn't fantastic any longer, it's inevitable. The inevitable is what you're doing or have done. The fantastic is simply what you didn't do. That goes for everybody.

The inevitable, the obvious, the expected. . . . They watch you, their faces like masks, set in the eternal grimace of disapproval. I always knew that girl was. . . . Why didn't you do this? Why didn't you do that? Why didn't you bloody well make a hole in the water?

I dreamt that I was on a ship. From the deck you could see small islands – dolls of islands – and the ship was sailing in a dolls' sea, transparent as glass.

Somebody said in my ear. 'That's your island that you talk such a lot about.'

And the ship was sailing very close to an island, which was home except that the trees were all wrong. These were English trees, their leaves trailing in the water. I tried to catch hold of a branch and step ashore, but the deck of the ship expanded. Somebody had fallen overboard.

And there was a sailor carrying a child's coffin. He lifted the lid, bowed and said, 'The boy bishop,' and a little dwarf with a bald head sat up in the coffin. He was wearing a priest's robes. He had a large blue ring on his third finger.

'I ought to kiss the ring,' I thought in my dream, 'and then he'll start saying "In nomine Patris, Filii...."'

When he stood up, the boy bishop was like a doll. His large, light eyes in a narrow, cruel face rolled like a doll's as you lean it from one side to the other. He bowed from right to left as the sailor held him up.

But I was thinking, 'What's overboard?' and I had that awful dropping of the heart.

I was still trying to walk up the deck and get ashore. I took huge, climbing, flying strides among confused figures. I was powerless and very tired, but I had to go on. And the dream rose into a climax of meaninglessness, fatigue and powerlessness, and the deck was heaving up and down, and when I woke up everything was still heaving up and down.

It was funny how, after that, I kept on dreaming about the sea.

5

Laurie said, 'I've had a peach of a letter from Ethel. She says you owe her money – two weeks' rent. And she says you've spoilt her eiderdown and a picture and the white paint in the bedroom and – my God, she does go on. I don't see why she wants to tell me about it. Here's the letter, anyway.'

227, Bird Street, W.
March 26th, 1914

My dear Laurie:

I expect by this time you know that Anna left this flat last week. Well, it's true that I had to ask her to go, but I hope you will not take any notice of the things she will tell you about me, because I have my side of the question too. Let me tell you that when I asked Anna to come and live with me I did not know what sort of a girl she was and she is a very deceiving girl. I know what life is and I do not want to be hard on anybody. So when she first started having Mr Redman to see her I did not say anything about it. He was a very nice man and he knew how to behave. But after he left she really overstepped all bounds but not in any way that you could respect because there are ways and ways of doing everything. It is one thing for a girl to have a friend or two but it is quite another for it to be anybody who she picks up in the street and without your leave or by your leave and never a word to me. And sulky my God. I have never seen a girl like that – never a joke or a pleasant word. And to crown it all last week she came to me and said she was going to have a baby. It appears to me from what she says that she must be nearly three months gone. When I told her she should have spoken to me before if she wanted me to help her – Why did you not do something about it before I said – she said I have been trying everything I ever heard of and thought you might know of something else. With her eyes staring out of her head looking quite silly. You get a desperate feeling it is awful she said. And when I said I think this is a bit much to ask me – won't he help you out – she said I do not know who he is and started laughing quite brazen and that just shows the sort of girl she is because there are ways and ways of doing everything aren't there. And all the time being sick and I said to her I cannot have this sort of thing going on in my flat and you cannot blame me either can you. And if you had only seen the state she left her room and I want to have somebody else there next week. A picture I had – the glass all smashed and there is the picture without a glass and the beautiful silk eiderdown spoilt with wine-stains all over it. That cost me 35/- and then it was cheap. And burns of cigarettes all over the place on the white paint. I am ashamed of the room now and it was such a beautiful room when she came in – all freshly done up. You can be mistaken about people – that is all I have got to say and have to pay for it. Besides she owes me two weeks money. Five guineas. I know she will come to you sooner or later with a lot of lies and I cannot bear to think that she will come to you like that because you are the sort of girl I think a lot of and I can tell you that I cannot afford to lose money like that either. If you knew the sort of girl she is I do not think you would have anything to do with her. She is not the sort of girl who will ever do anything for herself.

Yours affectionately
Ethel Matthews.

Hoping to see you soon. And my landlord has complained about her too.

'I don't know why she should write all that to you,' I said.

Laurie said, 'I don't know either.'

'You shouldn't give people a handle like you do,' she said. 'If you give people a handle they'll always take it.'

'I don't owe her any money,' I said. 'It's the other way round. She borrowed nearly three quid from me and she never paid it back. I don't know why she should write all that to you.' And all the time thinking round and round in a circle that it is there inside me, and about all the things I had taken so that if I had it, it would be a monster. The Abbé Sebastian's Pills, primrose label, one guinea a box, daffodil label, two guineas, orange label, three guineas. No eyes, perhaps. . . . No arms, perhaps. . . . Pull yourself together.

My hands were getting cold and I knew I was going to be sick again.

'I know of somebody,' Laurie said. 'But whether she'll do it for you now is another question. It's a thing that can happen to anybody, but you really ought to have done something about it before. I could have told you that all that business of taking pills is no good. . . . Those people who sell those things – they must make a pot. . . . I don't know whether she'll do it for you now. Have you got any money?'

'Yes,' I said. 'I sold my fur coat. I could give her ten quid.'

'It's not enough,' Laurie said. 'She won't do it for that. My dear, she'll want about fifty. Don't you know anybody who'll lend it to you? What about that man you talked about who used to give you money? Won't he help you? Or were you kidding about him?'

'No, I wasn't kidding.'

'Well, why don't you write to him?' she said. 'Because I warn you if you go on much longer you won't be able to get it done at all. Why don't you write now? I've got some awfully nice note-paper and you can use it. People go a lot by note-paper. When you're asking for money you don't want to give people the idea that you're down and out, you want to puzzle them a bit.'

'Say you're ill and ask him to come and see you,' she said. 'And give him my address; it's better than asking him to a bed-sitting-room. And for God's sake cheer up. It'll be all right.'

'I don't know what to say,' I said.

'Don't be a fool. Say Dear Flukingirons, or whatever his bloody name is. I'm not very well. I'd like very much to see you. You always promised to help me. Etcetera and so on.'

From a long way off I watched the pen writing: 'My dear Walter ...'

6

The big tree in the square opposite d'Adhémar's flat was perfectly still, and the forked twigs looked like fingers pointing. Everything was perfectly still, as if it were dead. Then a bird chirped anxiously and they all started – first one, and then another, and then another.

'Listen to that. The poor little devils think it's night,' Laurie said.

'And you can't blame them,' d'Adhémar said.

She had told me, 'He's slightly potty, but an awfully sweet old thing. And he's got a lovely flat and he says he's just bought a marvellous book of dirty pictures.'

I liked him, but he put scent on. I could smell it, and the wine in my glass. The awful thing was that, even when I wasn't feeling sick, I knew it was always just round the corner, waiting to start again.

After lunch he walked up and down the room reciting a poem which began: 'Philistins, épiciers'; and then he talked about Sunday in London; and about the Portobello Road, which was near his flat; and the streets round it, the dead streets, and the blank faces of the houses.

'It's terrible,' he said, waving his hands about. 'The sadness, the hopelessness. The frustration – you breathe it in. You can see it; you can see it as plainly as you see the fog.' He laughed. 'Never mind. Let's look on the bright side of things. Of course, frustration can become something homely, desirable and warm.'

'Go on, Daddy,' Laurie said, 'don't drivel. Show us your book of dirty pictures.'

We looked at a book of drawings by Aubrey Beardsley.

'I'm disappointed,' Laurie said. 'Very disappointed. I don't call that hot stuff. Is that book really worth a lot of money? All I can say is, some people don't know what to do with their money.'

It was a quarter to four. I said, 'I must go now.'

'What time's he coming?'

'At half past four.'

'Have a cognac before you go,' d'Adhémar said. He poured the brandy into three small glasses. 'Here's to the smug snobs and the prancing prigs and the hypocrites and the cowards and the pitiful fools! And then who's left?'

'She'd better not drink; it makes her sick,' Laurie said.

I got a taxi outside.

(Of course it'll be all right. Something will happen when I'm better, and then something else, and then something else. It'll be all right.)

He was late, and while I was waiting I was very nervous. I kept swallowing the lump in my throat and it kept coming back again. Then the bell rang and I went to the door and opened it.

I said, 'Hullo, Vincent,' and he smiled at me and said, 'Hullo.' I took him into the sitting-room.

'Walter wrote and told you I was coming?'

'Yes, he wrote from Paris.'

'Is this your flat?' he said, looking round.

'No, I'm staying here with a friend – Miss Gaynor. It's her flat.'

'I'm awfully sorry to hear you haven't been well,' he said. 'What's the matter?' When I told him he sat forward in his chair and stared at me, looking very fresh and clean and kind, his eyes clear and bright, like blue glass, and his long eyelashes never still for a second. He stared at me – and he might just as well have said it.

'Oh, I don't mean it's Walter's. I don't know whose it is.'

He leaned back in the chair again and didn't speak for a bit. Then he said, 'Of course Walter will help you. Of course he will, my dear. You needn't worry about that. Of course he will. What do you want to do?'

'I want not to have it,' I said.

'I see,' he said. And he went on talking, but I didn't hear a word he was saying. And then his voice stopped.

I said, 'Yes, I know. Laurie's told me of somebody. She wants forty pounds. She says she must have it in gold. She won't take anything else.'

'I see,' he said again. 'All right; you shall have the money. Don't fash yourself; don't be miserable any more.' He took my hand and patted it.

'Poor little Anna,' making his voice very kind. 'I'm so damned sorry you've been having a bad time.' Making his voice very kind, but the look in his eyes was like a high, smooth, unclimbable wall. No communication possible. You have to be three-quarters mad even to attempt it.

'You'll be all right. And then you must pull yourself together and try to forget about the whole business and start fresh. Just make up your mind, and you'll forget all about it.'

'D'you think so?' I said.

'Of course,' he said. 'You'll forget it and it'll be just as though it had never happened.'

'Will you have some tea?' I said.

'No, thanks, I won't have any tea.'

'Then have a whisky-and-soda.'

I had one too – it didn't make me feel sick, for a wonder – and while we were drinking he told me he knew of somebody who had had it done and she had said that it was nothing much, nothing to make a fuss about.

I said, 'It's not that that I make a fuss about. It's that sometimes I want to have it and then I think that if I had it, it would be a ... It would have something the matter with it. And I think about that all the time, and that's what I mind.'

Vincent said, 'My dear girl, nonsense, nonsense.'

'I can't understand it,' he said. 'I simply can't understand it. Was it money? It can't have been money. You must have known that Walter would look after you. And he'd fixed everything up. He was awfully worried when you went off and didn't let him know where you were. He said several times how worried he was. He'd fixed everything up.'

'So much every Saturday,' I said. 'Receipt-form enclosed.'

'It's no use talking like that. You're going to be pretty glad of it now, aren't you?'

I didn't answer.

'Is this going to be your address? Shall we write here? Are you going to stay on here with your friend?'

'Only for the next four or five days.'

'Then where will you be?'

I said, 'I don't know exactly. Laurie's told me of a flat going in Langham Street.'

'D'you know what the rent is?'

'It's two pounds ten a week.'

'That'll be all right. You'll be able to manage it.' He coughed. 'About the forty pounds – when d'you want it?'

'I'll have to see her first – Mrs Robinson, I mean. I'll have to see her first and find out.'

'Quite,' he coughed again. 'Well, you must let me know. When you write, write to me – not to Walter. He's going to be abroad for some time.'

'Thank you very much,' I said. 'You're awfully kind.'

He looked at Laurie's photograph on the mantelpiece. 'Is this your friend?' he said. 'Is she as pretty as that?'

'Yes, she's pretty,' I said.

'I'm sure I've seen her about somewhere.'

'I daresay you have,' I said. 'She's got a lot of friends; you'd be surprised.'

'She really is pretty. But hard – a bit hard,' as if he were talking to himself. 'They get like that. It's a pity.'

'By the way,' he said, 'there's just one thing. If you have any letters of Walter's I must ask you to give them to me.'

'I'm sorry, I must insist on that,' he said.

I went and got the letters. I didn't look at them, except the one on the top, which was, 'Will you be in a taxi at the corner of Hay Hill and Dover Street at eleven to-night? Just wait there and I'll pick you up. Shy Anna, I love you so much. Always, Walter.'

'Are these all?' Vincent said.

'They're all I kept,' I said. 'I don't keep letters as a rule.'

'There's the one he wrote from Paris, too, saying you were coming – you'd better have it as well.' I took it out of my handbag and gave it to him.

'You're a nice girl, you really are. Now, look here, don't go getting ideas into your head. You've only got to make up your mind that things are going to be different, and they will be different. ... Are you sure these are all the letters?'

'I've told you so,' I said.

'Yes, I know.' He pretended to laugh. 'Well, there you are. I'm trusting you.'

'Yes, I see that.'

'Where are you going when you leave here?' I said.

'Who – me? Why?'

'Because I'd just like to know. Because I can't imagine what you're going to do when you leave here and I like to be able to imagine things.'

'I'm going into the country,' he said. 'Till Tuesday morning, thank God.'

'What do you do?'

'I play golf and so on.'

'How nice!' I said. 'How's Germaine?'

'Oh, she's all right. She's gone back to Paris. She doesn't like London.'

'It must be lovely in the country.'

He said, 'It smells good.'

'You told me about it,' I said, 'in your letter.'

'What letter? Oh yes, yes, I remember.'

'It's no use asking me for that one,' I said. 'It wasn't one I kept.'

'Look here, cheer up,' he said. 'It's going to be all right for you. I don't see why it shouldn't be all right for you.'

When Laurie came in I was crying. She said, 'Oh, for God's sake, what's the good of crying? Have you fixed it up all right?'

'Yes,' I said.

'Then what is there to cry about?'

D'Adhémar was with her. He said. 'T'en fais pas, mon petit. C'est une vaste blague.'

7

The bedroom in Mrs Robinson's flat was very tidy, and there was some mimosa in a vase on the table.

She came in, smiling. She was Swiss – French-Swiss.

I said, 'Elles sont jolies, ces fleurs-là.' Simpering, wanting her to know that I could speak French, wanting her to like me.

She said, 'Vous trouvez? On me les a donnés. Mais moi, j'ai horreur des fleurs dans la maison, surtout de ces fleurs-là.'

She was tall and fair and fat and very fresh-looking. She was dressed in red, close-fitting. Not in very good taste, considering she was so fat. I thought, 'She doesn't look a bit French.' I gave her the money sewn up in a little canvas-bag. I didn't know gold was so heavy.

She smiled and nodded and moved her hands, telling me about what I ought to do afterwards. That was the only thing French about her – that she moved her hands a lot.

She brought me a small glass of brandy. I said, 'I thought it was rum they had.'

'Comment?'

I drank it very quickly, but it didn't go to my head at all. I kept telling myself, 'She's awfully clever. Laurie says she's awfully clever.'

She went away and I shut my eyes. I didn't want to see what she was doing. When I felt her standing near me again I said, 'If I can't bear it, if I ask you to stop, will you stop?'

150

She said, as if she were talking to a child, 'Oh, yes, yes, yes, yes, yes. ...'

The earth heaving up under me. Very slowly. So slowly.

'Stop,' I said. 'You must stop.'

She didn't answer. I couldn't move. Too late now to move, too late.

She said 'La,' blowing out her breath.

I opened my eyes. I went on crying. She went away from me. I sat up and everything was different. She brought me my handbag. I got out my handkerchief and wiped my face.

I thought, 'It's all over. But is it all over?'

She said, 'That will be all right. In two weeks, three weeks.'

'But it's quite sure?'

'Yes, quite sure.'

She smiled and said politely, 'Vous êtes très courageuse.' She patted me on the shoulder and went out and I got dressed. Then she came back and took me to the door and shook hands with me at the door and said, 'Alors, bonne chance.'

I got outside. I was afraid to cross the street and then I was afraid because the slanting houses might fall on me or the pavement rise up and hit me. But most of all I was afraid of the people passing because I was dying; and, just because I was dying, any one of them, any minute, might stop and approach me and knock me down, or put their tongues out as far as they would go. Like that time at home with Meta, when it was Masquerade and she came to see me and put out her tongue at me through the slit in her mask.

A taxi passed. I put my hand up and the man stopped. I couldn't get the door open and he got down and opened it for me.

Laurie was waiting for me in the flat in Langham

Street and when I came in she said, 'Well, has the first part of the programme gone off all right?'

'Yes,' I said. 'She says I've just got to wait and it'll be all right. She says I must walk about as much as I can and wait; and not do anything – just wait, and it'll be all right.'

'Well, I should do just what she says. She's very clever.'

'I'll wait for a bit,' I said. 'But I hope I shan't have to do it for very long. I don't think I'll be able to stand waiting for it to happen for very long. Could you? She said was I alone at night? It would be better not.'

'Well, why not ask that charwoman, Mrs What's-her-name, to stay?'

'Mrs Polo.'

'What a name! Why not ask Mrs Polo to stay?'

'She can't. She's got a baby. Besides, I think I'd better not mix her up in it.'

'That's right,' Laurie said. 'It's just as well not to mix anybody else up in it. You'll be all right. That woman's very clever.'

'Yes, I know. It's only waiting for it to happen that I mind.'

Laurie said, 'Well, anyhow I should go slow on the gin if I were you. You've been taking too much lately.'

The flat was full of furniture and pink curtains and cushions and mats with fringes. Very swanky, as Maudie would say. And the *Cries of London* turned up too, but here in the bedroom.

Everything was always so exactly alike – that was what I could never get used to. And the cold; and the houses all exactly alike, and the streets going north, south, east, west, all exactly alike.

Part Four

I

The room was nearly dark but there was a long yellow
ray coming in under the door from the light in the passage.
I lay and watched it. I thought, 'I'm glad it happened
when nobody was here because I hate people.'

I thought, 'Pain ...' but it was so long ago that I had
forgotten what it had been like. I was all right, except
that every now and again it was as if I were falling
through the bed.

Mrs Polo said, 'It was like this when I come this evening and I didn't know what to do, so I rung you up, miss.
And I don't want to be mixed up with a thing like this.'

'But why ring me up? It's nothing to do with me,'
Laurie said. 'You ought to have got a doctor.'

Mrs Polo said, 'I thought she wouldn't want a doctor
here asking questions. She told me it come on at two
o'clock and it's nearly eight now. Supposing anything
'appens and there's a row.'

'Oh, don't be a fool,' Laurie said. 'She'll be all right.
It's bound to stop in a minute.'

'Are you all right?' she said.

'I'm a bit giddy,' I said. 'I'm awfully giddy. I'd like a
drink. There's some gin in the sideboard.'

'She oughtn't to have anything to drink now,' Mrs Polo
said.

Laurie said, 'You don't know anything about it. A
drink won't do her any harm. Champagne – that's what
they give them; champagne's what she ought to have.'

I drank the gin and listened to them whispering for a

long while. Then I shut my eyes and the bed mounted into the air with me. It mounted very high and stayed there suspended – a little slanted to one side, so that I had to clutch the sheets to prevent myself from falling out. And the clock was ticking loud, like that time when I lay looking at the dog in the picture *Loyal Heart* and watching his chest going in and out and I kept saying, 'Stop, stop,' but softly so that Ethel wouldn't hear. 'I'm too old for this sort of thing,' he said; it's bad for the heart.' He laughed and it sounded funny. 'Les émotions fortes,' he said. I said, 'Stop, please stop.' 'I knew you'd say that,' he said. His face was white.

A pretty useful mask that white one watch it and the slobbering tongue of an idiot will stick out – a mask Father said with an idiot behind it I believe the whole damned business is like that – Hester said Gerald the child's listening – oh no she isn't Father said she's looking out of the window and quite right too – it ought to be stopped somebody said it's not a decent and respectable way to go on it ought to be stopped – Aunt Jane said I don't see why they should stop the Masquerade they've always had their three days Masquerade ever since I can remember why should they want to stop it some people want to stop everything.

I was watching them from between the slats of the jalousies – they passed under the window singing – it was all colours of the rainbow when you looked down at them and the sky so blue – there were three musicians at the head a man with a concertina and another with a triangle and another with a chak-chak playing There's a Brown Girl in a Ring *and after the musicians a lot of little boys turning and twisting and dancing and others dragging kerosene-tins and beating them with sticks – the masks the men wore were a crude pink with the eyes squinting near together squinting but the masks the women wore were* made of close-meshed wire covering the whole face and tied at the back of the head – the handkerchief that went over the back of the head hid the strings and over the slits for the eyes mild blue eyes were painted then there was a small straight nose and a little red heart-shaped mouth and under the mouth another slit so that they could put their tongues out at you – I could hear them banging the kerosene-tins.

'It ought to be stopped,' Mrs Polo said.
'I'm giddy,' I said. 'I'm awfully giddy.'

I was watching them from between the slats of the jalousies dancing along dressed in red and blue and yellow the women with their dark necks and arms covered with white powder – dancing along to concertina-music dressed in all the colours of the rainbow and the sky so blue – you can't expect niggers to behave like white people all the time Uncle Bo said it's asking too much of human nature – look at that fat old woman Hester said just look at her – oh yes she's having a go too Uncle Bo said they all have a go they don't mind – their voices were going up and down – I was looking out of the window and I knew why the masks were laughing and I heard the concertina-music going

'I'm giddy,' I said.

I'm awfully giddy – but we went on dancing forwards and backwards backwards and forwards whirling round and round

The concertina-man was very black – he sat sweating and the concertina went forwards and backwards backwards and forwards one two three one two three pourquoi ne pas aimer bonheur supreme – the triangle-man kept time on his triangle and with his foot tapping and the little man who played the chak-chak smiled with his eyes fixed

Stop stop stop – I thought you'd say that he said

My darling mustn't worry my darling mustn't be sad – I thought say that again say that again but he said it's nearly four o'clock perhaps you ought to be going

You ought to be going he said – I tried to hang back but it was useless and the next moment my feet were groping for the stirrups – there weren't any stirrups – I balanced myself in the saddle trying to grip with my knees

The horse went forward with an exaggerated swaying lilting motion like a rocking-horse – I felt very sick – I heard the concertina-music playing behind me all the time and the noise of the people's feet dancing – the street was in a greenish shadow – I saw the rows of small houses on each side in front of one of them there was a woman cooking fishcakes on an iron stove filled with charcoal – and then the bridge and the sound of the horse's hoofs on the wooden planks – and then the savannah – the road goes along by the sea – do you turn to the right or the left – the left of course – and then that turning where the shadow is always the same shape – shadows are ghosts you look at them and you don't see them – you look at everything and you don't see it only sometimes you see it like now I see – a cold moon looking down on a place where nobody is a place full of stones where nobody is

I thought I'm going to fall nothing can save me now but still I clung desperately with my knees feeling very sick

'I fell,' I said. 'I fell for a hell of a long time then.'

'That's right,' Laurie said. 'When he comes tell him that.'

The bed had gone down to earth again.

'Tell him you had a fall,' she said. 'That's all you've got to say. . . .'

'Oh, so you had a fall, did you?' the doctor said. His

hands looked enormous in rubber gloves. He began to ask questions.

'Quinine, quinine,' he said; 'what utter nonsense!'

He moved about the room briskly, like a machine that was working smoothly.

He said, 'You girls are too naïve to live, aren't you?'

Laurie laughed. I listened to them both laughing and their voices going up and down.

'She'll be all right,' he said. 'Ready to start all over again in no time, I've no doubt.'

When their voices stopped the ray of light came in again under the door like the last thrust of remembering before everything is blotted out. I lay and watched it and thought about starting all over again. And about being new and fresh. And about mornings, and misty days, when anything might happen. And about starting all over again, all over again . . .

PENGUIN (🐧) CLASSICS

www.penguinclassics.com

- *Details about every Penguin Classic*

- *Advanced information about forthcoming titles*

- *Hundreds of author biographies*

- *FREE resources including critical essays on the books and their historical background, reader's and teacher's guides.*

- *Links to other web resources for the Classics*

- *Discussion area*

- *Online review copy ordering for academics*

- *Competitions with prizes, and challenging Classics trivia quizzes*

PENGUIN CLASSICS ONLINE

READ MORE IN PENGUIN

In every corner of the world, on every subject under the sun, Penguin represents quality and variety – the very best in publishing today.

For complete information about books available from Penguin – including Puffins, Penguin Classics and Arkana – and how to order them, write to us at the appropriate address below. Please note that for copyright reasons the selection of books varies from country to country.

In the United Kingdom: Please write to *Dept. EP, Penguin Books Ltd, Bath Road, Harmondsworth, West Drayton, Middlesex UB7 0DA*

In the United States: Please write to *Consumer Sales, Penguin Putnam Inc., P.O. Box 12289 Dept. B, Newark, New Jersey 07101-5289.* VISA and MasterCard holders call 1-800-788-6262 to order Penguin titles

In Canada: Please write to *Penguin Books Canada Ltd, 10 Alcorn Avenue, Suite 300, Toronto, Ontario M4V 3B2*

In Australia: Please write to *Penguin Books Australia Ltd, P.O. Box 257, Ringwood, Victoria 3134*

In New Zealand: Please write to *Penguin Books (NZ) Ltd, Private Bag 102902, North Shore Mail Centre, Auckland 10*

In India: Please write to *Penguin Books India Pvt Ltd, 11 Community Centre, Panchsheel Park, New Delhi 110017*

In the Netherlands: Please write to *Penguin Books Netherlands bv, Postbus 3507, NL-1001 AH Amsterdam*

In Germany: Please write to *Penguin Books Deutschland GmbH, Metzlerstrasse 26, 60594 Frankfurt am Main*

In Spain: Please write to *Penguin Books S. A., Bravo Murillo 19, 1° B, 28015 Madrid*

In Italy: Please write to *Penguin Italia s.r.l., Via Benedetto Croce 2, 20094 Corsico, Milano*

In France: Please write to *Penguin France, Le Carré Wilson, 62 rue Benjamin Baillaud, 31500 Toulouse*

In Japan: Please write to *Penguin Books Japan Ltd, Kaneko Building, 2-3-25 Koraku, Bunkyo-Ku, Tokyo 112*

In South Africa: Please write to *Penguin Books South Africa (Pty) Ltd, Private Bag X14, Parkview, 2122 Johannesburg*

BY THE SAME AUTHOR

After Leaving Mr Mackenzie

After being left by Mr Mackenzie (and not the other way around) Julia faces facts. But standing on her own is more difficult than she thought – she is restricted by the very existence she has created. *After Leaving Mr Mackenzie* is a brilliant, yet brutal, portrait of a woman struggling to retrieve both life and love.

'One of the finest British writers this century' A. Alvarez

Good Morning, Midnight

Jean Rhys was a talent before her time with an impressive ability to express the anguish of young, single women. In *Good Morning, Midnight*, Rhys created the powerfully modern portrait of Sophia Jansen, whose emancipation is far more painful and complicated than she could expect, but whose confession is flecked with triumph and elation.

'Her eloquence in the language of human sexual transactions is chilling, cynical and surprisingly moving' A. L. Kennedy

Quartet

Set against a background of winter-wet streets and smoke-filled cafés, Jean Rhys's first novel is both poignant and disturbingly intimate in its vivid depiction of a woman on her own.

'She is loved not just for a talent that seems as spontaneous and individual in its personality as physical beauty, but for a special kind of courage' *Guardian*

Wide Sargasso Sea

Inspired by Charlotte Brontë's *Jane Eyre* and drawing upon memories of her own Caribbean childhood, this classic study of betrayal is Jean Rhys's brief, beautiful masterpiece.

'Rhys took one of the works of genius of the 19th century and turned it inside-out to create one of the works of genius of the 20th century' Michèle Roberts, *The Times*